HOME TO YOU

ST. CLAIR FAMILY SERIES

BOOK TWO

ERIN STEVENSON

Happy Jack Publishing

Copyright © October 2018
by Erin Stevenson Quint

Cover photo courtesy of Town + Country Cedar Homes
http://www.cedarhomes.com/

Cover Design by Tina Lampe

ISBN: 1-944104-20-8
ISBN-13: 978-1-944104-20-7

1

"DADDY, SHELBIE DROPPED her sippy!"

If April hadn't announced it so clearly, Shelbie's ear-piercing scream would have alerted Brandon St. Clair that something had gone very wrong in the back seat. He tried to make eye contact with his daughters in the rearview mirror, but could only see their shadowy outlines in the darkness.

"April, honey, we're almost to Uncle Landon's," he said. "Can you—" then he stopped himself. *You were about to ask a 4-year-old to climb out of her car seat to get her sister's sippy cup off the floor, while you're whizzing along the interstate at 65 miles an hour? What kind of lousy dad are you?*

Brandon switched the windshield wipers to *high* as the rain pelted down even harder. He could barely see, and it was pitch black. He consulted his phone in its dash holder, guiding him to his brother's house in suburban St. Louis. Thank God, they would be there in sixteen minutes. It was almost midnight.

He had fully intended to be there long before now, but

everything that could go wrong at the hospital had gone wrong today. He'd had to cover for another doctor, and the surgical schedule was backed up. So much for Fridays being a lighter day.

By the time he'd picked up the girls from the sitter's, gotten them fed (with yet another fast-food meal), and arrived home to pack for the trip, they were already well behind schedule. Then Brandon realized he hadn't put the last load of the girls' laundry into the dryer last night, so he had to make a decision: delay their start by another hour, or take the damp clothes with them?

A trash bag filled with damp clothes rested next to their suitcases in the back.

A flash of lightning and simultaneous crash of thunder shook the vehicle, and Brandon tightened his grip on the wheel while easing his foot from the gas.

"Daddy, I'm scared!" April cried.

"I want Mommy!" Shelbie screamed.

I want Mommy, too, Brandon thought as he blinked back tears. *Oh God, why, why did you take her?*

2

MORGAN ANDERSON RESTED her chin on her hand and gazed at her sister. "Motherhood totally suits you," she said with a smile.

Kelsea St. Clair lifted her sleeping daughter up to her shoulder and rubbed her back. "It's the most exhausting thing I've ever been through, but I love every minute of it."

Her husband, Landon, entered the room. "I'm not so sure we love it at three in the morning," he quipped, with an affectionate squeeze of his wife's shoulder. He held out his arms. "You want me to take her?"

"Sure, thanks," Kelsea replied, and Morgan watched as they made the seamless transfer. She tried to ignore the way that her sister and Landon operated as one mind, one heart. Morgan swallowed, and turned her attention back to the baby.

"She's really out," she commented. Little Rose hadn't made a peep.

Kelsea yawned and looked up at her husband. "How's Isaac?"

"Fine. Hopefully he'll sleep a few hours before he needs to eat again."

Morgan was so proud of her sister. "You're really brave, nursing twins. But it's the best thing for them. Good for you."

Kelsea looked at Landon. "Have you heard from Brandon?"

"Yeah, they should be here in about fifteen minutes." He left the room with the baby.

Morgan glanced at her phone. "Oh, gosh, is it that late already?" She'd lost track of the time, as was usually the case when she and Kelsea got together. Morgan had driven down from Chicago and thankfully arrived before the spring storm.

She had never met Landon's brother, but knew about the tragic car accident that had taken his wife early last summer. "You know, it's kind of weird that I've never met Brandon," Morgan mused. "You and Landon have been together over three years now, and I've spent some holidays with you."

Kelsea put her chin in her hand. "Well, we really haven't seen him that much, either. When Darla was still alive, one of them was always on call, or she was pregnant with one of the girls or had just given birth, or something."

"So, what's the schedule for the weekend?" Morgan asked. "Or have you figured that out yet?" She stifled a laugh.

Kelsea feigned indignance. "Hey, I'm getting better! But I don't have a printed itinerary like you would," she teased. They both laughed. Kelsea was famous for flying by the seat of her pants. Morgan and their mom were the planners in the family.

"Mom will arrive sometime tomorrow afternoon," Kelsea said. "Landon and Brandon's parents will be here sometime then, too. We'll all go to the Spaghetti Factory for dinner tomorrow night, and then church on Sunday, and a barbeque back here."

"Don't forget the babies' dedication service," Morgan said.

"Of course! The whole reason you're all here," Kelsea said with a smile. "I *love* the outfits you got them to wear. They're just precious."

"Well, they're the most beautiful babies in the world, and I'm the proudest aunt ever!" Morgan had discovered that she absolutely loved shopping for baby clothes.

Kelsea reached over and squeezed Morgan's hand. "Thank you." Her expression turned serious. "Be honest with me. Does it bother you at all—you know—"

"What? To see you being a mother? Kels, no! Not at all. I'm so happy for you and Landon. I adore the babies, and *love* being an aunt." Kelsea had been her rock when Morgan discovered that she would probably never be able to have children.

Silence settled itself over the two sisters like a warm blanket, and Morgan's heart began to quicken. *I guess this is as good a time as any.* "Kels, I, um—I need to tell you something." She took a deep breath. "I—oh wow, this harder than I thought it would be."

Worry settled over her sister's dark brown eyes. "Morgy, what's wrong? Are you sick again? Are you—"

Morgan shook her head adamantly. "Oh, no—I'm fine. I didn't mean to scare you. It's just—" she took another breath. "I've been thinking about maybe adopting a baby."

Kelsea's jaw dropped, and her eyes grew large. She grabbed Morgan's hand. "Oh, Morgy, that's fantastic!" Her eyes teared up.

"Yeah, well—" Morgan gave a nervous little laugh and tucked a strand of hair behind her ear. "It's such a big step, but I'm not getting any younger, and I'll probably never get married, and even if I do, I still can't—well, you know."

Kelsea squeezed her hand. "You don't know that, Morgan," she said softly. "But what got you thinking about this?"

Morgan wiped a wayward tear from her eye. "Well, you know I've been working with that arts program with preschoolers in Chicago," she said. Kelsea nodded. "There are so many children who need a loving home. A lot of the children in the program are orphans, and it just got me thinking. You and I are both big advocates for adoption." One of their best friends from high school was adopted, and they both knew other families who had adopted children.

Morgan shrugged. "Anyway, you know me and my planning." The two sisters laughed together. "So just pray for me, that God will make His will clear on this. It's a huge decision."

"I sure will," Kelsea said warmly.

Morgan chewed her lower lip. "And keep it to yourself for now, okay?"

"Of course."

"Now, back to this weekend," Morgan said, closing the door on that subject. "When do the guests of honor arrive? I can't wait to meet them."

Kelsea's eyes lit up. "Rosie and Ike's flight gets in at eleven-thirty tomorrow morning. I can't wait to see them. It's been more than a year." Rose and Ike Goldman owned a resort on a Caribbean island where Landon and Kelsea had met, and had become like family to the young couple. "I hope you're okay staying at Maggie and Mike's with them," she added, referring to hers and Landon's best friends who lived across the street.

"Of course," Morgan said. "They have plenty of room for all of us, and I'll be there to help Rosie and Ike if they need it."

"Maggie practically begged me to house some of you there! I wanted you here, but Landon thought it would be better for his brother and the girls to be close to us." She looked at Morgan apologetically.

Morgan reached out and touched her sister's hand. "Kels, you don't need to apologize. I know it's a difficult situation. How's he doing, anyway?"

Kelsea shook her head. "Not great. He's super-doctor-in-control at work, and a hot mess otherwise."

"Does he have any help with the girls, other than daycare?"

"No, he's determined to handle the home front on his own. And he's still so broken and lost without Darla. I think Landon and their parents are going to try to talk with him this weekend."

"Well, I should probably get back to Mike & Maggie's," Morgan said. "They gave me the front door code and said to stay here as long as I wanted to." She stood, and Kelsea got to her feet and held her arms out. The two sisters hugged.

"I'm so glad you're here, Morgy," Kelsea whispered.

Morgan snorted softly and pulled back. "You know you're the only one who's allowed to call me that, don't you?" She looked into her sister's dark brown eyes and smiled.

"Yes, and you're the only one who can call me Sissy," Kelsea replied with a smile.

A bright bolt of lightning flashed outside, illuminating the living room window, and the women held their breath, bracing themselves. Still, they both jumped when a crack of thunder boomed a mere second later.

And then, the lights flickered out.

"Gosh, that's close!" Morgan exclaimed, her hand on her chest.

Landon's voice called out, "Honey, don't move. I'm coming with flashlights." The sisters huddled together until he arrived.

"Are Penny and Sheldon okay?" Kelsea's Pomeranians had been a big part of her life even before she met Landon.

He came into the room. "They're fine. They're completely zonked out on our bed."

Kelsea looked at Morgan. "Maybe you should stay here," Landon held out a flashlight.

"I'll be fine. It's just across the street," Morgan replied. She put her hand up. "Guys, I'll be fine."

Kelsea walked with her to the front door, and opened it. "Oh, wow, it's pouring!" She quickly reached into the hall closet. "Here, at least take this," she said, and handed Morgan a big umbrella.

"Thanks, I think I'll need it." She squeezed Kelsea's hand. "Love you, see you tomorrow."

"Yes, come for pancakes around nine. Oh! Would you babysit so Landon and I can go to the airport?"

You can do this. "I'd love to!" Morgan grinned.

"Thanks! Sleep well, Morgy."

3

BRANDON COULDN'T THINK of anything but getting off the road and out of the rain. He was so tired, and he had a headache. That last crack of thunder ushered in a chorus of wailing from his young daughters, which only added to the pounding in his head. The lightning must have hit a transformer, because all the lights around them went out.

He'd turned his phone off because it was almost dead. *LaBonne Terrace,* that's what he was looking for. Had Landon told him it was the first house on the left, or the right, after the road curved? Brandon came to an intersection and slowed to try to read the sign. He couldn't really see it, but it looked like it might begin with an *L,* so he turned right. He knew he was probably going a little too fast, but there were no other cars on the road, and he just wanted to get there.

"Big Victorian house with a circular driveway," he repeated his brother's instructions to himself. Brandon looked left, hardly able to see anything in the downpour.

As he looked right, a sudden movement flashed in the headlights, and he instinctively slammed on his brakes. Was it an animal? Brandon's mouth dropped open and his heart leapt into his throat. He clutched the steering wheel as his heart pounded in his ears.

An indistinguishable figure, hunched under an umbrella, dashed across the road just in front of the SUV.

I almost hit someone. The idiot just ran out in front of me, didn't even look! The realization sent white-hot anger racing through his veins. Without thinking, he rolled down his window.

"Hey!" He screamed. "What is WRONG with you?"

The figure slowed, but didn't stop, and the person's head was almost totally obscured by the umbrella. He was medium height, but that's all Brandon could make out.

"Where do you think you are, the Indianapolis Speedway?" a woman's voice shouted.

I almost hit a woman.

Water poured in through the window. Brandon quickly rolled it up, his breath coming in short bursts. April and Shelbie continued wailing.

"Girls, we're almost there," he said over his shoulder, *I hope,* he added to himself. Brandon wished he could get them out of their car seats to comfort them.

When he looked back to the front windshield, the woman was gone. Surrounded by the darkness and the pouring rain, he had no idea which way she had gone. Brandon rested his forehead on the steering wheel. "Oh, God, help me." He put his foot back on the gas pedal and inched forward, struggling to see.

Almost immediately, he glimpsed a driveway on the right, and swung out in a slow, wide arc. His headlights illuminated a big, Victorian house. *Finally.* Brandon's grip on the steering wheel loosened, and he pulled up to the front door. He put the car in park and closed his eyes. "Thank you, Lord," he whispered.

The door opened, and there was his brother with a big umbrella. Landon came right up to the car, and Brandon lowered the passenger window. "Hey, man," he said, relief flooding his veins. The girls had finally stopped screaming.

"Hey, man," Landon answered back. "Sorry, I just have the one umbrella. How can I help?"

"Maybe get the girls in the house first?" He turned in his seat and reached over to unbuckle April. "This is Uncle Landon, April, remember him?"

With his brother's help, Brandon had both girls and the car unloaded in minutes. As soon as he crossed the threshold into the house, the lights flickered back on.

"Hey, perfect timing!" Landon exclaimed.

Kelsea came into the entryway and held out her arms. "I'm so relieved you're here! I've been praying that you'd arrive safely." Brandon gave her a hug, and she stooped down to greet the girls. "April and Shelbie, you're both getting so big!" She held out a hand to each girl. "Why don't you come with me and have a snack while your daddy and Uncle Landon put your things upstairs?"

Brandon was amazed at his sister-in-law's ability to assess a situation and do exactly the right thing. He picked up his roller bag, the girls' suitcase. His brother reached for the toy bag and another bag of the girls' things.

"What's this?" Landon said, pointing to the black trash bag.

Brandon winced. "Oh, it's clean laundry that didn't make it into the dryer."

"Okay, we'll leave it here and take care of it when we come back down," Landon replied. Brandon was relieved that his brother didn't judge him.

Landon led him up the stairs, down the hall, and into a large blue and white bedroom with a queen-sized bed and an inflatable mattress on the floor, piled with blankets and pillows. "You can figure out the sleeping arrangements," he said.

Brandon had never been so happy to see a bed in his life. "The girls will probably want to sleep with me tonight," he said. "This is terrific, thanks."

"You have your own bathroom," Landon said, pointing to a door. He paused and studied Brandon as if seeing him for the first time. "You okay? How was the drive?"

Brandon let out a breath and rubbed a hand through his dark hair. "It was a long day. I did four surgeries this morning." He stretched and stifled a yawn. "The drive was okay until the last hour. It kept raining harder and harder. And then I almost hit one of your idiot neighbors. I don't know what she was doing out in the middle of the night, but she ran right out in front of the car."

Landon frowned. "Neighbor? Just now?" Brandon nodded. "Oh, that wasn't a neighbor. That was Kelsea's sister, Morgan. She's staying across the street with our friends Mike and Maggie. She left just before you got here." He turned and began walking toward the door into the hallway.

Brandon followed him. "Well, she's an idiot," he muttered.

"Do you want to see your niece and nephew?" Landon said with a smile.

"You bet!" Brandon answered. He couldn't believe his brother had both a son and a daughter now. He followed Landon into a softly lit nursery where two white cribs resided.

"This is my son, Isaac," Landon said proudly, resting his arms on the first crib.

Brandon felt his chest swell on his brother's behalf. "Oh, man, he's so little!"

Landon laughed softly. "He's huge! Four months old now."

Brandon felt a wave of sadness wash over him. "I can't remember the girls being this small." He turned to the other crib with Landon.

"And here's Rose Elizabeth," Landon said tenderly.

"Look at all that dark hair," Brandon murmured. "Like her mama."

Landon smiled. "She has her mama's personality, too. Sassy." He leaned down and rested his hand on the baby's head. He looked at Brandon. "There's nothing like it," he whispered.

Brandon nodded and swallowed past the lump in his throat. "They're beautiful, bro."

They went back downstairs into the kitchen and found the girls enjoying bowls of cereal with Aunt Kelsea.

"We're having breakfast, Daddy!" April exclaimed.

"I like the marshmallows," Shelbie said around a mouthful of cereal.

"Wow, that looks good," Brandon said.

Kelsea laughed. "Help yourself," she said, indicating several assorted boxes on the counter. Landon got out a bowl, a spoon, and the milk.

"Are we having cereal for breakfast in the morning, too?" Brandon asked with a smile.

"No, we're having your brother's famous pancakes," Kelsea said. She sidled up to Landon and looked at him lovingly, and their arms went around each other. A jolt of pain sliced through Brandon's heart.

They chatted for a few more moments and then he took the girls upstairs and got them ready for bed. Brandon wished he could take a long, hot shower, but being in a strange place, it was more important for him to be there for April and Shelbie. He'd take his shower after they fell asleep.

Brandon climbed into bed with them, still in his clothes, and they snuggled in, one on each side. Shelbie popped her thumb in her mouth. What would he ever do without them? They were his world now. His thoughts went to Landon and Kelsea, their arms entwined around each other, and he missed Darla more than ever. Would the pain ever go away?

The next thing Brandon knew, it was morning.

4

MORGAN KNOCKED ON her sister's front door and poked her head in. "Knock, knock!"

Kelsea was just coming down the stairs, holding Isaac. "Good morning!" The dogs ran ahead of her, greeting Morgan with enthusiastic barks and yips.

"Morning, Sissy, morning, Penny and Sheldon." She patted their heads, deposited the umbrella in the corner, and held out her arms. "Come to Aunt Morgy, Isaac!"

Kelsea laughed as she handed the baby over. "Whatever happened to *no one else can ever call me Morgy!*?"

Morgan kissed the little boy's silky-soft cheek. "My niece and nephew can call me whatever they want." She tipped her head toward the umbrella. "I'm returning that. Thanks."

Kelsea put it in the closet. "Did you get soaked anyway? It was pouring so hard."

"No, but I almost got hit," Morgan replied.

"Hit?" Kelsea began walking toward the kitchen, and Morgan followed her.

"Yeah, some moron in an SUV came flying around the corner. I don't know what he was thinking."

Kelsea stopped. "Right when you left here?" Morgan nodded. "Oh gosh, that must have been Brandon. They drove in just after you left."

Morgan rolled her eyes. "Well, he's a moron." She followed Kelsea into the kitchen, and stopped.

Two adorable little blond girls sat at the counter, eating pancakes. Rose sat happily in the baby swing.

Landon stood at the island range top, over a griddle. A dark-haired man stood next to him, and they looked up in unison when the two women entered the room. Morgan's breath caught in her throat.

Kelsea had told her that they were always mistaken for twins, even though Landon was eleven months older. But Morgan had never seen anything like it. The two were like matching bookends. They were exactly the same height and build, with the same facial structure, the same amber-brown eyes, and even the same cleft in their chins that little Isaac had inherited. They had nearly identical haircuts, but whereas Landon's hair was blond, Brandon's was dark brown, almost black.

Both men had the same smile, showing perfect white teeth. "Morning, Morgan," Landon said.

His brother's smile dimmed noticeably. *Great.*

"Good morning," she managed.

"This is my sister, Dr. Morgan Anderson," Kelsea said cheerily. "Meet Dr. Brandon St. Clair."

That's right, he's a surgeon. So he's Dr. *Moron.* Morgan shifted little Isaac in her arms as she watched the wheels turning in Dr. St. Clair's head. His smile warmed up a little.

He dipped his head in acknowledgement. "Doctor," he murmured. He held out a plate on which Landon piled a half dozen golden pancakes.

"Nice to meet you," Morgan said softly. Suddenly she felt very self-conscious, like she always did in the presence of a good-looking guy. *Stop it,* she scolded herself. *He's not that handsome.*

Liar! Another voice in her head shouted. *He's totally hot, and you know it!*

There was no doubt that Kelsea's husband was handsome, but in Morgan's opinion, his brother's dark hair took him to a whole new level. She had a real weakness for tall, dark, handsome men. Before Kelsea met Landon, she did, too. *TDH* was their code, and Brandon St. Clair had it in spades.

Morgan tried not to stare. She was so self-conscious and wanted to thrust her nephew into his mother's arms and bolt from the room. But she managed to stay where she was, rocking back and forth on the balls of her feet with Isaac and—hopefully—looking calm.

Kelsea held her arms out for the baby. "Let me take him so you can eat," she said.

"Um, oh, sure," Morgan said. She tucked a strand of her caramel-colored hair behind one ear and turned to the counter where she saw plates, silverware, and napkins.

As soon as she picked up a plate, Brandon materialized beside her with a spatula and plate of steaming pancakes. *Wow, is he ever tall.* Morgan was taller than average, but he dwarfed her.

"Here you go," he said, placing three pancakes on her plate.

"Oh, no, thanks, two is plenty," she said, and felt her face heating up. *Moron, moron,* she repeated to herself. She tried to ignore his sculpted chest and broad shoulders.

"You sure?"

She nodded.

He took one pancake back. "Okay, then," he said with a smile. Morgan swallowed.

Penny and Sheldon ran into the room, their expressions expectant. "No pancakes for you two," Landon scolded with a smile.

"Oh, they're so cute," the older girl said.

"Eat your breakfast, April," Brandon said. "You can play with the dogs later."

As Morgan picked up a fork and napkin, the smaller girl looked up from her pancakes and stared at Morgan. "You look like my mommy."

The plate that Brandon was holding clattered to the countertop, and it seemed as if the air went out of the room.

Morgan didn't know what to say. She glanced at Brandon, whose face had blanched white. Landon froze where he was.

Kelsea, still holding Isaac, moved to stand next to the little girl. "Shelbie, that's Morgan," she said matter-of-factly. "She's my little sister, just like you're April's little sister. She looks a little like your mommy, doesn't she? But she's taller, and her eyes are green instead of blue." Kelsea looked at her brother-in-law. "Brandon, could you bring Shelbie and April some more juice?" Then she made eye contact with her sister. "Morgan, come and eat your pancakes before they get cold."

Morgan walked quietly to the table while holding her breath, and sat down.

"I want apple juice this time, please," Shelbie said. Morgan glanced at Kelsea and Landon, who seemed to be holding their breath as well. It appeared that the awkward moment had passed.

Brandon cleared his throat. "Sure thing, Shelbie. And good job saying please."

Morgan was sure the pancakes were delicious, but she didn't taste a thing.

Brandon took the carton of apple juice out of the fridge and turned to the counter. He frowned. "Where's April?" he asked.

The other adults looked around. "She was just here," Kelsea said. She looked at her husband and Morgan. "Did either one of you see her leave?"

"No," Morgan and Landon said in unison.

Brandon set the carton down on the counter. "I have a feeling I know what this is about," he said, his face grim. He turned and abruptly left the room.

When he returned a few moments later, he didn't say anything, just fixed a plate of pancakes and sat down.

"Is everything okay?" Landon asked.

Brandon didn't reply. He motioned to the butter dish on the other side of Kelsea. "Would you please pass the butter?"

"Sure," Kelsea murmured. She glanced at Landon and then at Morgan and Brandon. "So, you're both doctors," she said brightly. "Brandon is an orthopedic surgeon."

Brandon took a sip of his juice and looked at Morgan. "What's your specialty?" he asked.

Morgan swallowed. *Here it comes.* She sat up a little straighter. "I'm a PhD. I'm an art therapist."

Brandon stared at her for a moment. He chewed a bite of

pancakes and swallowed. "So, what's that? Painting and drawing?"

Morgan started to open her mouth to retort, but her sister jumped in. "Morgan is an Assistant Professor at the Midwest Art Institute in Chicago. She's one of the youngest faculty ever hired there, and has published tons of research."

Brandon gave Morgan what felt like a placating smile. "Well, that's impressive," he said. Everyone continued eating for several moments.

"Honey, these pancakes are amazing," Kelsea said. It sounded to Morgan that her sister was trying to fill the awkward silence.

"They sure are, bro." Brandon stood, put his plate in the sink, and picked up his younger daughter. "Let's get you cleaned up and dressed," he said.

"Thanks for breakfast," he tossed over his shoulder as he carried Shelbie out of the room.

Landon let out a breath. "Morgan, I'm sorry—"

Morgan shook her head. "It's okay, Landon."

"He's just—he's not himself." He sighed. "I think I know what's up with April. She's not handling the loss of her mother well. I'm sure Shelbie's comment upset her."

Morgan's heart gave a painful squeeze. "She's only four. Of course she's not handling it well." She rested her chin on her hand and sighed. "Poor little thing." She looked from Kelsea to Landon. "Do I—do I really look like their mother?"

Landon frowned. "I don't think so. But then again, I've known Darla since we were all teenagers. Your hair color is similar, though."

Kelsea nodded. "Yes, it's really close, and it's long and

straight, too. In the grand scheme of things, you look a lot more like her than I do. I could see where a three-year-old would make the connection." She lifted Rose out of the baby swing and kissed the top of her head. "April has always had a more sensitive spirit. She's a thinker. Shelbie is more easy-going. And she doesn't remember Darla as clearly as April does. She just has a general impression of her. "

The three adults sat silent for a moment, each lost in their own thoughts. Landon stood and began gathering the breakfast dishes. "I'll get everything cleaned up here."

"Hey, Morgan," Kelsea said, "could you get Isaac out of his swing and bring him upstairs? I'll get these two fed before we have to leave for the airport." She paused. "If you're still willing to babysit?"

As long as I can steer clear of Dr. Moron. Morgan pasted a smile on her face. "Are you kidding?" she said, "I can't wait!"

5

BRANDON SAT DOWN on the bed and ran a hand through his hair. *Great.* He was stuck here for a family weekend with a woman who reminded Shelbie of her mother, and was a PhD to boot. He had never had a good impression of people with doctorates. He'd met several over the years—among them his cousin, Mark—who thought they had the biggest brains in the room. He had a PhD in Psychology and insisted that everyone call him "Doc." Brandon sneered. Mark probably made his wife call him that, even when they were alone.

He and Darla used to have good-natured arguments about it. Her best friend had a PhD, so she didn't have the same bias toward them. And Dar loved everyone and always wanted to give them the benefit of the doubt—even Mark. Brandon squeezed his eyes shut. How were he and the girls ever going to get over losing her?

When April had disappeared from the kitchen, Brandon found her upstairs on the bed, curled up in a ball. She wasn't even crying. She was just lying there, staring into space. His heart broke for his older daughter. What was he going to do? His beautiful, sunny, and gentle April Dawn was losing her spirit. She would take one step forward and two steps back.

Brandon didn't have a clue how to help her. Heck, he was barely holding himself together. He and Darla had agreed that no matter the demands of their careers, that they would raise their children themselves. No nanny or au pair, like most of their friends and colleagues had. Since Darla's death, Brandon's folks kept telling him to hire someone to help, but he stood firm. Putting his daughters in daycare five days a week and leaving them with neighbors when he was called in on emergencies was bad enough.

For once, he wished that he had family close. His parents lived in Wisconsin, about four hours away. Darla's folks lived in Arizona, along with her two sisters and their families. His and Landon's younger sister, Sara, was in college in Michigan. Their older sister, Reagan, lived in Miami.

The girls were looking out the window at the backyard. "Daddy, I want to swing!" Shelbie shouted as she jumped up and down. Brandon stood and looked over their heads to the large yard below. Even though his brother's twins weren't ready for it, a large, colorful play structure sat in the middle of the lush green grass.

"Let's get you dressed, then," Brandon said, and lay Shelbie down on the bed to change her diaper. That was something else he needed to figure out, how to potty train her. Darla had taken complete charge of that with April. He'd heard somewhere that summer was the optimum time to attempt it, so he was waiting.

April dressed quietly, and Brandon asked if she wanted

him to fix her hair. She shook her head no, and he decided not to press her about it. He handed her a brush, which she ran haphazardly through her hair while he got Shelbie's up into two pigtails.

"I hafta have the purple bows, Daddy," she instructed with all seriousness.

After he got that detail taken care of, Brandon ushered the girls into the hallway and toward the stairs, but Shelbie stopped and pointed the opposite direction. "I wanna see the babies," she said in a loud whisper.

Brandon smiled. "We have to be very quiet. I think they're sleeping."

"I be quiet."

April nodded, too. They tiptoed into the nursery, and Brandon picked both of the girls up to peer into the cribs. "Here's baby Rose," he whispered.

"Baby Wose," Shelbie parroted. "I wuv you, Baby Wose."

He turned to the other crib. "And baby Isaac."

"Brother?" Shelbie asked.

"Yes, Isaac is Rose's brother."

Shelbie's little forehead wrinkled up as she frowned. "My brother?"

"No, you don't have a brother. Isaac is your cousin."

"I wish I had a brother." Brandon was surprised to hear those words come out of April's mouth.

Then he felt Shelbie's little hands on his cheeks.

"I want brother, too, Daddy," she ordered.

A little piece of Brandon's heart broke off. He adored his daughters, and had hoped someday to have a son, too. Now he knew he'd have to let go of that dream.

He forced a smile. "Maybe someday God will give you a brother," he said. He didn't know what else to say. Then he gave each girl a peck on the cheek and set them down. "Come on, let's go check out the backyard."

6

MORGAN SAT IN the family room looking out at the backyard. She'd seen and heard everything that had just transpired in the twins' room over the baby monitor.

Shelbie skipped into the room ahead of her father and sister. "We're going to get a brother someday!" she cried. *Oh, to have the faith of a child.* Shelbie stopped in front of Morgan and put her hands on her hips. "I forgetted your name."

Morgan took in Shelbie's purple shoes, pants, and hair ribbons. Her shirt was white with purple and lavender hearts. She was just the cutest thing, with her blond pigtails bobbing up and down. Morgan smiled. "I'm Morgan. And I'll bet your favorite color is purple." She looked at April. "What's your favorite color, April?"

Brandon stepped forward. "Ah—we don't call adults by their first name, girls."

Morgan stood up. "Then you can call me Dr. Anderson."

Brandon frowned. "You can call her *Miss* Anderson." He quickly stepped to the French doors and slid the screen door open. "Girls, go on and play for a few minutes. I'll be right there."

Really? Miss? This guy was unbelievable. Morgan mentally prepared herself for battle. "You're kidding me, right?" she said as Brandon turned to look at her.

"No, I'm not kidding. I want to raise my daughters to respect adults."

Morgan itched to cross her arms over her chest, but forced them to stay down at her side. "And what's disrespectful about calling me by my title?"

Brandon smiled in a way that bordered on a grimace. "I don't want them to be confused. I'm a doctor. Their mother was a doctor. In their world—our world—a doctor is someone in the medical field."

Morgan felt her blood boiling. *Of all the*—she'd met a few doctors like this in her practice. Fortunately, they were more the exception than the norm. She let out a huff. "How—how are you even Landon's brother?" Landon was a partner at the largest, most successful law firm in St. Louis, and he was still one of the kindest, most down-to-earth people she had ever met.

Brandon looked completely confused. "What does Landon have to do with this?" He parked his hands on his hips. "I'm one of the top orthopedic surgeons in Minneapolis—in the Midwest, in fact—and I worked extremely hard for over a *decade* to earn the title of *doctor.* It just riles me that anyone who goes to college for a few years and publishes a couple of articles can run around making everyone call *them* 'doctor' and misleading everyone."

Morgan could hardly believe what she was hearing. She

drew in a deep, cleansing breath through her nose and straightened her spine. *"Dr.* St. Clair, I know that medical doctors pride themselves on the depth and breadth of their knowledge. But in the hour and a half that I've known you, you've shown me that you're really very ignorant. You possess little to no knowledge about what it means to be a doctor of philosophy, or anything about the widely recognized and *respected* field of art therapy."

A squawk from the baby monitor cut her off. She marched out of the room, her back ramrod straight. Then she stopped and turned to him. "And you obviously don't have any kind of a degree in *driving,*" she added.

She stomped up the stairs to the nursery, her breathing coming in angry spurts. *TDH* or not, Brandon St. Clair had an abrasive, unpleasant personality. Morgan had no idea how she was going to survive the weekend without punching his lights out.

She crept into the nursery, and both babies were sleeping soundly. Morgan stood for a long time over Isaac's crib, and then over Rose's. As she stared at her sister's children, a wave of tenderness washed over her. She fingered one of her niece's dark curls. Kelsea and Morgan had been so very different growing up, but the one dream they always shared was to be mothers. Morgan had taken their father's death especially hard, and dreamed of having a husband and children of her own someday. But that day hadn't yet come, and she felt that dream slipping away, especially after her diagnosis.

Morgan heard a child laughing, and stepped to the window that overlooked the backyard, where Brandon was pushing his daughters on the swings. He looked exhausted and it was only mid-morning. Morgan felt a pang of sympathy for him. She couldn't imagine what it would be like to lose your spouse and have to raise two young children alone, especially juggling a demanding, high-pressure career.

Then she remembered his haughty, condescending words and attitude, and her sympathetic thoughts dissolved. She crossed her arms and continued staring down at him. He'd probably love it if she stayed in the house the whole time Kelsea and Landon were gone so he wouldn't have to deal with her.

Morgan turned on her heel and went back downstairs. She knew exactly what she was going to do.

7

BRANDON PUSHED SHELBIE and April on the swings. "Higher, Daddy!" Shelbie shouted. This girl was going to love roller coasters once she discovered them. He had a feeling Shelbie's teen years would be one long, wild ride.

He tamped down a feeling of guilt. He had no idea why he'd come down so hard on Morgan Anderson, or why she got under his skin. He thought about her. Maybe she did remind him a little bit of Darla. Morgan was quite a bit taller, and was a completely different body type, but their coloring was similar. All he knew was that he didn't want to be around her. Thankfully, his parents would arrive later today, along with Kelsea's mom and their other special friends, and that would make it easier to avoid Morgan.

"I want to get down, Daddy," April said. He slowed her swing to a stop, and she hopped off and wandered off toward a plot of dirt that looked like it might be a future garden.

Great. Here came Morgan. The two Poms trailed after her. Why couldn't one of the babies have needed something so she could stay inside, out of his hair? She smiled, sat down in one of the patio chairs, and set the baby monitor on the table.

"It's beautiful out here, isn't it?" she called. She lifted her face to the sky and drew in a deep breath. "I love the days after big storms have moved through and cleared the air."

Brandon grunted and continued pushing Shelbie. Morgan was apparently planning on staying out here. He wondered if he should take the girls into the house.

April was crouched in the grass near a plot of moist dirt, playing with a stick. Last night's wind had littered the yard with them. Morgan got up and went over to her, and sat down on the grass with her. "Whatcha doin'?" Brandon heard her ask.

"Drawing," April replied in a soft voice.

"Do you like to draw?" April nodded. "I do, too," Morgan added. She picked up another stick and Brandon saw her start to doodle in the dirt.

They just sat there, and Brandon thought they talked occasionally, although he couldn't hear what they said. He was lost in thought when he heard Shelbie say, "Daddy! I said stop!" He stilled her swing and she jumped off and ran over to join her sister and Morgan.

"Hi, Shelbie," Morgan said. "We're drawing. Would you like to draw, too?"

Shelbie shook her head and placed her hands on her hips. "No, I'm going to pick up all the sticks." She dramatically drew out the word *all*. Shelbie started skipping through the yard, singing and gathering sticks as she went. Penny and Sheldon trailed after her, and she babbled to them and threw sticks for them to run after.

Brandon smiled to himself. April was like Mary in the

Bible, content to immerse herself in quiet reflection for long periods of time. Shelbie was Martha, all busyness, all the time. His gaze swept across the large yard. Picking up sticks could keep Shelbie busy for several hours, but she'd soon tire of the task and look for something else to do.

Feeling awkward, Brandon sat down at the round patio table. After a few minutes, Shelbie ran over to her sister. "April, you hafta help clean up the yard!" she exclaimed.

"I'll come in a minute, Shel," she said.

Shelbie huffed and skipped away, resuming her task. Pretty soon, she was back, and April agreed to help this time. Morgan got up and headed his way. "You have quite a little artist there," she said as she sat down.

Brandon ignored her comment. "Just for the record," he said sternly, "I have an impeccable driving record. I do just fine until some—" he almost said *idiot* but tried to temper himself. "Some person with no common sense comes running out in front of me."

"I have plenty of common sense. You were driving too fast. End of story." She plowed on. "That's in the past, so let's put it aside and talk about your daughter's artistic flair."

Brandon frowned. "Artistic flair?" he looked at Morgan evenly. "She was messing in the dirt with a stick."

"She drew a picture of your family at the mountains," Morgan said. "It was quite good and it was meaningful to her." She paused. "Did you take a trip to the mountains?"

Brandon swallowed. Memories overtook him and he wondered if he could draw his next breath.

"Yes," he croaked. His voice broke, and he cleared his throat. They had gone skiing in Utah last spring. It was their last trip together as a family, but no way was he going to share that. He needed to take control of this conversation right now. He had no intention of breaking down in front of Morgan Anderson.

Brandon sat up straighter and leveled her with a hard look. "How do you determine that something scratched into the dirt with a stick is 'quite good'?"

"The level of detail, both what I could see and what she told me. Her fine motor control is remarkable for a child of that age. I'd love to see what she does with colored pencils or crayons."

Brandon stood. "Well, that's nice, but she's not your research subject." He turned his back on her and began to walk away.

"Just what do you have against me, Dr. St. Clair?" Morgan called out sharply.

He turned back and blew out a breath. "Look," he said, "we have to get through this family weekend, so let's just coexist peacefully and shelve the attitude for the sake of your sister and my brother. Deal?"

Morgan jumped to her feet and put her hands on her hips. "Shelve the attitude?" she said in a voice laced with disbelief. She narrowed her eyes at him. "Physician, heal thyself!"

Morgan watched the high-and-mighty *Dr. St. Clair* pick up some larger branches and interact with his daughters, laughing with them and giving them an occasional hug or pat. She crossed her arms over her chest. Really, it wasn't fair that such an insufferable boor should be so handsome and so…masculine. She had to admit that he seemed to be a good dad. She recalled Kelsea's comment about him being a control freak at work, and totally falling apart at home.

Many doctors that Morgan had dealt with were alpha personalities who felt the need to be in control, some to the extent of having a "god" complex. She'd gone on one dinner date with one handsome, charming resident who insisted on ordering for her as if she were incapable of doing it for herself. Morgan had quickly set him straight on that, and he never called her again.

The baby monitor continued to show that all was well upstairs, and Morgan sat contentedly in the sun until she heard Landon call out, "hi, we're here!" That sent Penny and Sheldon into full bark mode.

"Hi, Unca Landon!" Shelbie squealed. She ran to him and launched herself up into his arms.

Morgan stood, and Landon laughed as April and Brandon joined them. Morgan stared at the older couple who stood next to her brother-in-law, dwarfed by him, Brandon, and even herself. They couldn't be more than a couple of inches over five feet.

"Meet Rose and Ike Goldman." Landon made the introductions, and everyone shook hands.

Shelbie looked at Rose. "My favorite color is purple," she said. "And I think your favorite color is pink!"

Everyone laughed. Kelsea had told Morgan about Rose's penchant for pink. Today, she wore a tie-dyed pink shirt with hot pink capris and her trademark pink Converse. Ike seemed quiet and pleasant, but Morgan could tell that a vibrant *joie de vivre* oozed out of Rose's every pore.

"Yes, indeed it is," Rose agreed, all smiles.

"You even have pink hair! Shelbie exclaimed, eyeing the

pink highlighted tips of Rose's white hair. "Daddy! Can I get purple in my hair?"

Everyone laughed again. "Ah, not now, Shelbie. Maybe when you're all grown up, if you still want to do that."

Shelbie wriggled out of Landon's arms, and he set her down. "Unca Landon, we cleaned up the *whole* backyard!" she said, sweeping one little arm in a wide arc in front of her.

"You did a great job, girls! Thank you," Landon said.

"Daddy helped with the big branches," April added.

"Let's go wash our hands, girls," Brandon said, ushering them into the house.

They heard Shelbie chattering happily as they walked away. "She has pink glasses, too! Daddy, can I get purple glasses?"

The Goldmans and Landon laughed along with Morgan. Rose reached up to adjust her pink-encrusted rhinestone glasses. "Your nieces are delightful," she said.

"They sure are," Landon agreed.

Everyone's attention turned to the baby monitor as it began to make noise, and Kelsea's voice came over. "Landon, could you or Morgan come help me?"

"I'll go," Morgan said, and quickly left.

She helped Kelsea dress the twins, and carried Rose downstairs while Kelsea took charge of Isaac. Everyone was in the family room, and Morgan handed her niece to Landon. Rose and Ike got settled on the couch, and she felt her eyes well up as her sister and brother-in-law tenderly laid the babies in their arms. She knew how much the older couple meant to them.

Morgan was so focused on the touching scene that she started when she heard Brandon's soft voice near her ear.

"Do you have your phone? Mine's upstairs. Could you get some pictures of this?"

His aftershave or cologne smelled wonderful, and Morgan resisted the urge to draw in a deep breath. *Moron, moron.*

She drew her phone from her pocket. "Of course, yes. Good idea." For once, Brandon had a pleasant, even tender, look on his face. Of course, he was focused on the babies, not Morgan.

Morgan spent the next several minutes taking pictures of the Goldmans with the babies and Landon and Kelsea, and tried unsuccessfully to forget that Brandon was there. Morgan hadn't ever let a man's physical attributes outweigh a sincere and kind heart and pleasant personality, things that meant much more, and that appeared to be totally lacking in Brandon St. Clair. Morgan was totally disgusted and frustrated over her hyperawareness of him.

Rose Goldman beamed as she looked down at her namesake. "This girl is going to do great things," she announced. "She may even grow up to be president."

"What about Isaac?" her husband countered with a smile. "Look at that strong profile. I think he'd make a great president, too."

"He can be Rose's vice president," she replied firmly. Everyone laughed.

After a few moments, Ike looked over at baby Rose. "I'm ready to hold that little beauty," he said, and Kelsea and Landon got the babies switched.

"Landon, this little boy is the spitting image of you—and your brother," Rose said. "You two aren't twins, though?"

"No, I'm almost a year older," Landon said.

"And I have a perfect nose," Brandon said with a smile aimed at his brother. *He really is perfect,* Morgan thought to herself. *Why can't he have a tooth missing, or a big wart on his nose, or hair sprouting out of his ears?*

Landon burst out laughing and touched the bump on his nose. "Kelsea thinks it gives me character." He looked at the Goldmans. "I got it in a hockey brawl in my misspent youth."

After a little while, Rose looked at April and Shelbie. "I think these girls would like to hold their little cousins. If it's okay with their parents," she added.

"Of course," Kelsea said, and they got the girls settled in with the babies. April and Shelbie were so excited, and Morgan took lots of pictures. Both girls got a turn at holding each twin with help from their dad.

Shelbie touched a gentle finger to little Isaac's cheek. "God is going to give us a brother someday." she announced.

Isaac began to fuss, and Brandon picked up his nephew and stood, gently bouncing him in his arms. He looked totally at home holding a baby, but a look of discomfort took over his features. "I don't know why she's obsessed with having a brother," he said softly.

"Sometimes, children know these things," Rose said.

"Well, it's not going to happen," Brandon said. He handed Isaac off to Landon. "Excuse me," he said as he left the room.

8

BRANDON WALKED QUICKLY through the family room, down the hallway and out the front door. He paced back and forth on the porch and rammed his hands through his hair, drawing in deep breaths.

Why, God? Why, why, why? Shelbie's talk of wanting a brother filled him with desperation for all that he had lost, for all the years ahead that he and Darla should have had. Raw anger and deep, piercing pain radiated through his chest. He braced his hands on the porch railing and hung his head. *God, how will I ever survive? I could easily be on this earth for fifty more years. Alone. I can't do it, God, I can't.*

Suddenly, Landon materialized at his side. Brandon hadn't even heard the door open.

"You okay, man?"

Brandon couldn't speak around the lump in his throat. Even if he wanted to sugar-coat things, this was the one person on this earth who could see straight through him. He shook his head and swallowed. "No, no I'm not," he whispered. Landon reached over and gave his shoulder a comforting squeeze. Brandon swiped at his tear-filled eyes. "I can't do this. I can't."

"I know," Landon said. "You can't. Not on your own." He sighed. "We're all worried about you. Let us help."

Brandon gave a mirthless laugh. "I'm sure Mom has some kind of intervention planned for this weekend. Are the girls coming, too? Strength in numbers?" He knew that Landon caught the reference to their sisters.

"No, Sara's got finals next week, and Reagan's tied up, the way Reagan always is." Their older sister worked at the *Miami Herald,* and was totally career-focused. Landon squeezed his shoulder again. "How are things with you and God?"

Brandon shook his head. "I talk with Him a lot. I talk *at* Him a lot," he corrected. "I keep asking *why,* but I never get an answer." He thought for a moment. "I'm still angry."

"That's normal." Landon's eyes were filled with compassion, not condemnation.

"But I'm stuck in the anger phase," Brandon said. "I can't get past it."

Landon moved on his other side and propped his hip against the porch railing. "Try this. You're angry because you can't change the outcome."

"Hmph," Brandon mused. "The physician's god complex?"

Landon nodded. "And you're still consumed with guilt. Am I right?"

No one else could have said that to Brandon and gotten away with it. He felt the same sick sensation that he'd wrestled with for almost a year bubble up in his stomach. He pressed a fist to his mouth. "I could have gone to the store that night, I *should* have—"

Landon looped a long arm around his shoulder. "You

could have. But you didn't send Darla out because you were a bad husband. You had a rare night off and wanted to stay home and put your girls to bed. And you can't change that. Bro, You. Can't. Change. It." Landon removed his arm. "You'll never move on until you leave the land of would-a could-a, should-a."

Brandon rubbed his eyes and let out a huge breath. "We've gotten through all the 'firsts.' First Thanksgiving, Christmas, birthdays, anniversary without her. This will be our first Mothers' Day," he said. He felt his eyes filling up again. "I don't know what to do, how to handle it. I don't know what's best for the girls." He looked at Landon.

"I know," Landon said. "So let your family handle it. Let us be there for you. We'll get you through it. I think Kelsea has some ideas."

Brandon managed a weak smile. "Your wife is very special," he said.

"Don't think I don't know it," Landon replied. "I'm very blessed. And you're blessed, too, even though you're still overwhelmed by grief. It's hard to see."

Brandon nodded. "I'm so tired of being tired. And discouraged. And not having any hope of getting past it."

Landon squeezed his shoulder. "You'll get past it. One step at a time, bro." He tilted his head toward the door. "You ready to go back in?"

Brandon shook his head.

Landon looked at him. "Could I pray with you?"

Like that will do any good, Brandon thought to himself. But this was his best friend in the world, so he nodded, and bowed his head.

9

"DO YOU HAVE a platter or something I can set these on?" Morgan was helping Kelsea with lunch. She was in charge of the sandwiches, and Kelsea was putting the finishes touches on a relish tray.

Rose walked in, and Morgan couldn't help but smile. Even after two days of travel, she was a pink ball of energy.

"I wish you girls would let me help," she said. "I'm not as old and feeble as I look."

Morgan and Kelsea laughed. "Okay, Rose, get the chips out of the pantry," Kelsea said, pointing to a door. She set tubs of potato salad and pasta salad on the counter.

"She's adorable. They both are," Morgan whispered to Kelsea.

"I know," her sister whispered back.

Rose laid the bags on the large island counter and climbed up on a stool. "Tell me about yourself, Morgan."

"Well, I live in Chicago, and I'm an art therapist."

Rose smiled brightly. "Oh, Ike's nephew is from Chicago." Then Rose asked her some questions about art therapy, which Morgan was happy to answer.

"You're such a lovely young woman, Morgan," Rose said. "Are you dating anyone?"

Not another matchmaker. Morgan was used to this from well-meaning people. No doubt Rosie thought she was the perfect match for Ike's nephew. "No. I have extremely high standards, and the right man hasn't come along."

Rose nodded. "David isn't at all your type," she commented. Morgan and Kelsea exchanged an amused glance. "But there's someone out there for you. God will put him in your path when you least expect it."

"What about that doctor you went to dinner with a few weeks ago?" Kelsea asked.

Morgan made a face. "Dud," she said, giving a thumbs-down.

"What about Landon's brother?" Rose piped up. "He's a handsome man, and he needs someone."

"No. No, no, no," Morgan shook her head vehemently. She stopped when she saw the frown on Kelsea's face. Her sister had no idea that she and Brandon had clashed multiple times in the few hours they'd known one another.

"I mean," she back-pedaled, "He's not really my type." She felt her face growing warm.

"He's exactly your type, Morgy," Kelsea drawled.

Morgan looked at Rose. "Well, we live hundreds of miles apart," she said.

Rose waved a dismissive hand. "Oh, that's nothing to God," she said.

Morgan carried two platters of sandwiches to the kitchen island. "I'm really not interested," she said firmly. "I'm focused on my career right now." She looked to Kelsea for help, and fortunately, her sister radar was in good working order.

Kelsea brought out pitchers of tea and lemonade from the fridge. "Anyway, Rose, Brandon is still in deep mourning for his late wife. I don't think he's ready to move on yet."

Rose nodded. "He still needs time. But God will work it out so those sweet little girls can have a brother." She looked at Morgan again. "I'm sure of it."

Morgan really wanted this conversation to end. Even if she and Brandon St. Clair lived in the same city and somehow got past their intense dislike for one another, her fertility issues would ensure that April and Shelbie's wish for a brother would never come true.

Thankfully, the men and girls came in then, and things got wonderfully lively as they had lunch, and Morgan was happy that she could avoid Brandon. When they were cleaning things up, Landon went to take care of the laundry, and Kelsea asked Brandon if he would go out to the garage and get the extra tables and chairs that were out there, and take them out to the deck for tomorrow's barbeque.

"Sure thing, Kels," he said.

"Morgan can help you."

Morgan seethed inwardly. She gave her sister *the look* behind Brandon's back.

Brandon looked at her and then at Kelsea. "I'm sure I can handle it," he said as he walked toward the door to the garage.

"No, you can't. It'll take two people," Kelsea said.

"Then Landon can help me," Brandon said.

Kelsea stopped and looked between him and Morgan. "Is something going on with you two?" she asked.

"No!" Morgan and Brandon said in unison.

Morgan quickly walked to Brandon. "Let's go." He opened the door and she placed her hand on his back and shoved him through it.

When it closed behind them, he pulled away from her. "What is wrong with you?" he scowled.

"Nothing's wrong with me! You are the most exasperating person I've ever met!"

"I get along just fine with everyone else, which means that you're the problem!"

Morgan marched past him. "Let's just get the tables and chairs out of here and be done with it." She spied them behind some things and started to figure out the easiest way to get to them. She moved a lattice panel out of the way and began to move a stack of boxes, and caught a rake just before it fell over.

Brandon stood behind her with his hands on his hips. "What are you doing? You're going to get hurt."

"Well then, it's good that there's a *real doctor* here to take care of me!" He didn't reply, and she glowered at him. "Well, are you going to help, or not?"

Brandon closed his eyes and muttered something to himself. "Come on, move out of the way and let me get it."

The bickering continued for several minutes and they finally got one table free and carried it around the house to the back deck. Then they went back for the other table and the chairs, never speaking.

Morgan went back into the house and joined Kelsea, who was standing at the sink. Morgan squirted soap on her hands and began to vigorously wash them. "Kels, if that was some kind of cute trick to throw Brandon and me together, give it up!" she hissed.

Kelsea's mouth dropped open. "What are you talking about?"

Morgan tilted her head. "Seriously?"

"Sheesh, Morgan! Chill."

10

BRANDON HUGGED HIS brother and sister-in-law and got into the car. "Thanks for everything. We had a great time." They had stayed over until Monday morning and were headed back to Minneapolis. Fortunately, Morgan left yesterday afternoon to go back to Chicago. Brandon felt that he could finally relax without her there.

They had finally reached a truce and agreed that the girls could call her *Miss Morgy*. In his opinion, it was the silliest name on earth. He still couldn't figure out why April and Shelbie were so drawn to her. It annoyed him that they trailed after her all weekend, and insisted that she sit with them in church yesterday.

Even worse, when they were milling around after the service as Landon and Kelsea received congratulations from their church family, a woman greeted him and Morgan and remarked on what beautiful little girls "they" had. Without thinking, he'd replied curtly, "They're not hers, they're mine." The woman's face turned beet red and she slunk away. Brandon managed to hold his tongue when the second similar comment came. After that, he'd taken the girls to the car.

They had nearly cried when "Miss Morgy" left after the barbecue. Kelsea saved the day by suggesting that her friend, Maggie, take April and Shelbie across the street to her house to meet their new puppies. But that presented a new set of problems. It was bad enough that they'd already fallen in love with Penny and Sheldon, but when the girls came back, they begged Brandon to let them *each* take a puppy home.

Brandon had to be the bad guy and put his foot down. He could barely manage the household, the girls, and himself. The thought of adding one animal, let alone two, to the chaos that was his life was completely impossible.

They got through Monday morning traffic, cleared the city, and got on the interstate. The girls were content in the backseat with games, books, and snacks that Aunt Kelsea had supplied.

Brandon loved getting out on the open road to clear his head. As Landon had forewarned him, his parents had sat him down for a long talk yesterday afternoon. Brandon had gotten so used to carrying his heavy load alone, and their tender concern finally caused him to break down. His dad, Jim, was still working at his engineering job, but his mom worked part-time, and offered to come to Minneapolis for a week each month over the summer to help Brandon out. It was a pretty easy trip from their home in Wisconsin.

"What if Sara came to live with you for a while, like a nanny, to help with the girls?" Janice St. Clair suggested.

Brandon shook his head. "I can't ask her to do that." He refrained from adding that he already had two children and didn't need a third. Sara was twenty, but still a kid, in

Brandon's eyes. "Mom, she can't even cook," he added, trying to lighten the moment.

His mother started to open her mouth again, and Brandon's dad laid a hand on her arm. "Don't press, Jan. Give him some time to think it over." Then Jim St. Clair leaned over and kissed his wife's cheek. "Why don't you go find a grandchild or two to spoil?" he said with a smile.

Brandon's mom sniffed. "I know, I know, you want to have a man-to-man talk," she said. She stood and bent down to hug her younger son. "I love you, Brandon. Please let us help you," she whispered, and then she was gone.

"Thanks, Dad," Brandon said, wiping his eyes. "I really do appreciate your support, and Mom's."

Jim St. Clair wasn't a big talker, and they sat in companionable silence for a few moments. Finally, he spoke. "Maybe a change of scenery would do you good. Have you ever thought about taking a job in a different city?"

Brandon was surprised at his dad's suggestion. "No, that's never occurred to me," he said. "I like my work, and Minneapolis is home." He couldn't imagine himself living anywhere other than his and Darla's home, or raising the girls anywhere else.

His dad clasped his shoulder. "Something to think about, then. I know it would be hard, but maybe it would be good for you in the long run. Pray about it," he added.

Brandon thought about it as he drove. He wasn't praying much these days. He decided to challenge God. "If you have a different plan for me, I'm not going to go looking for it, so you'll need to bring it to my doorstep."

11

MORGAN CALLED HER sister. "I'm home," she said.

"Oh! Good. You usually text," Kelsea said. "I wasn't expecting you to call. How was the trip?"

"Okay," Morgan said. She grunted as she wrestled her suitcase up the stairs of her townhouse.

"Are you hurting, Morgy?"

Morgan stopped. Her sister had an uncanny ability to know when she was in pain.

"I'm okay. I'll get everything organized here and then take a pain pill." The condition that was at the root of Morgan's infertility issues was under control, and only flared up on occasion, usually when she'd overdone. It had been a big weekend.

"Me getting organized takes five minutes," Kelsea said drily. "It will take you two hours. Take it slow."

Morgan smiled. "Yes, mama." She changed the subject. "It was such a great weekend. The babies are so precious, and I loved every minute of it." *Well, except when Landon's conceited, detestable brother was around.*

"It was perfect. I'm so glad everyone was able to come."

"Rose and Ike are just adorable," Morgan said. She couldn't get the amusing picture of Rose in her Converse out of her mind. "They were so sweet with the babies."

"I know! They really are like family to us. I'm so glad all of you got to meet them." Kelsea giggled. "Promise not to get mad?"

"Mad? About what?"

"Before they left, Rosie took my hand and whispered into my ear, 'Your sister and that handsome doctor are going to make a beautiful couple.'"

"Aargh!" Morgan shouted. She rolled her eyes. "Not. Happening."

"Was something going on between you two?" Kelsea asked.

"No!" Morgan insisted. "Kels, I know you and Landon think he walks on water, but he was totally rude to me all weekend."

"I never saw that," Kelsea murmured.

"Well, that's how those kind of people are. They act one way to one person, and then show a completely different side to everyone else." Morgan unzipped her suitcase and started putting things away.

"You sure got along well with April and Shelbie."

Morgan's voice softened. "They're so precious. I enjoyed them so much." She sighed. "April has an amazing artistic ability, and I think art therapy could really help her sort through her feelings about her mom, but Dr. Moron wouldn't hear of it."

"Dr. Moron?!" Kelsea sputtered.

"Oh," Morgan said, "Sorry, that's just what I call him in my head."

"You sure have some strong feelings for him," her sister murmured. "You know, they say the line between hate and love is pretty thin."

"Not in this case! It's a brick wall. Make that a brick wall encased in steel. Case closed."

"Okay, I get it," Kelsea said. "So, what's your next step with looking into adoption?"

Morgan stilled. "I don't know, I just said I was thinking about looking into it." Suddenly, the idea seemed overwhelming. She sat down on her bed.

Her sister seemed to sense her hesitancy. "I'm sorry, Morgy, I shouldn't have brought it up. I'll be praying for you."

"Thanks, Sissy." They talked for a few more minutes, then said goodnight.

Morgan opened her laptop and transferred all the pictures from her phone onto it. Then she started scrolling through them. Her eyes teared up unexpectedly when she saw pictures of herself with her niece and nephew that Kelsea had taken. "I'd be a good mom, I know I would," she whispered to no one.

Then, her breath caught as the screen filled with a close-up shot of Brandon holding Isaac. *Who took this picture?* As far as she could tell, it had been taken out on the deck at lunchtime earlier that afternoon before Morgan had left. Morgan let out a huff and shook her head. It had to have been Kelsea, but Morgan wasn't going to call her out about it. Her sister would just deny it.

She continued to stare at the picture, and her heart

skipped a beat. *This* Brandon St. Clair was unbelievably handsome. All traces of the negative emotions that Morgan had witnessed on his face throughout the weekend were gone. He looked completely relaxed and happy, holding the baby close. Rose Goldman was right; little Isaac looked as much like his uncle as he did his dad.

Brandon was looking directly into the camera, and Morgan felt like he was looking straight into her soul. She closed the computer screen and walked away.

12

THREE MONTHS LATER

"CHICAGO? YOU'RE MOVING to Chicago?" Landon's jaw dropped.

Brandon laughed and adjusted the screen so he could unload the dishwasher. He and his brother were video chatting. "Sure am. You're talking with the new Medical Director of the Chicago Professional Sports Medicine and Orthopedic Center."

"Wow, bro. Well, congratulations."

"Thanks. It's brand new, the only one of its kind. The five professional sports teams in Chicago came together to plan it, build it, and fund it to serve all of their athletes. It's state of the art. Believe me, they've spared no expense."

"I hope they didn't spare any expense when it came to your salary," Landon said drily.

Brandon smiled, and named a figure.

"Are you kidding me?" Landon grinned. "That's almost the annual operating budget at the firm!"

Brandon laughed. It was an amazing salary, but he knew his brother was exaggerating. "Yeah, it's a game changer. I'll run the whole place, and get to pick my surgeries. They said I could do as few as three or four a week. I wasn't about to tell them that most days, I've usually done that many before noon."

"Any travel involved?" Landon asked.

Brandon nodded. "Some. I'm pretty sure I'll get comp tickets to attend championship games and the like."

"Wow, man. Take me to the Super Bowl with you."

"You got it, man." Brandon laughed.

Landon shook his head slowly. "I never thought you'd leave Minneapolis."

Brandon let out a breath. He was leaving the life that he and Darla had built together. "Yeah, when Dad floated the idea to me at your house, I was dead set against it. But about a month later, the attorney representing the Center called me out of the blue. I have no idea where he got my name. They gave me everything that I asked for. I really think this is the right move. The change will be good for the girls and me. And we'll be closer to Mom and Dad."

"And to us. I know that'll make Mom happy. Have you told them yet?"

"Nope." Brandon smiled. "You're the first. Always."

"So, when are you moving?"

"I start the day after Labor Day. Movers are coming on Thursday."

"Wow, that's fast. Have you sold the house yet?"

"I just listed it with an agent. My employers said they'd cover the payment for a year if it doesn't sell. But it will. It's a sellers' market here."

Landon whistled softly. "Hey, is Peanut going with you?" Their younger sister, Sara, had moved in with Brandon and the girls a couple of months ago. Their mother's suggestion had turned out to be a good one.

"Yeah, she's excited about it."

"How's that working out, her being the nanny and all?"

Brandon smiled. "Great, as long as she stays out of the kitchen." Landon laughed.

Brandon saw his brother's attention move away from the screen. Then Kelsea appeared, holding Isaac. "Hi, Uncle Brandon," she said.

"Whoa! Look at that linebacker! Hey, big boy!" Brandon laughed when Isaac's little face broke into a wet grin.

Landon picked up his son and bounced him in his arms. "Maybe one of those teams you're gonna work for will give Isaac an early tryout." His eyes darted to his wife. "Can we tell her?" he said in a stage whisper.

"Tell me what?" Kelsea said.

"Sure," Brandon replied. Landon made the proud announcement and Brandon supplied the details.

Kelsea beamed at him. "That's fantastic! I'm really happy for you, Brandon. Congratulations. Oh, my goodness, Morgan lives in Chicago! You'll have to get together."

Brandon tried to look enthusiastic at the prospect. "Yeah, we'll have to do that," he said.

There was a long, loud squawk off-screen, and Landon smirked. "Your daughter is calling you," he said to Kelsea.

"Gotta run, Brandon. Congrats again!" She waved at him and disappeared.

"Great," Brandon muttered. "I forgot that she was from Chicago." That really wasn't true, but he didn't want his brother to know that. Every once in a while, he thought about Morgan. About how her beautiful green eyes lit up when she was with the girls, and her gentleness with them. How intuitive she was about the best way to talk and deal with them. Then he would think about how she rubbed him wrong, and how he didn't want to examine the possible reasons why. And then, he would feel guilty for having treated her so badly. Since Brandon didn't deal well with guilt, he'd just shove her out of his mind. And until now, he thought the only time he'd ever see her was at some random and infrequent family event.

Landon peered in the direction his wife had gone, waited a beat, and then looked at the camera, right into his brother's eyes. "Don't worry, bro," he whispered. "I think the Windy City is big enough for both of you."

13

BRANDON LOOKED UP and did a full three-hundred-sixty-degree turn in the two-story foyer of his new home in one of Chicago's northwestern suburbs. They'd been here for three weeks and were finally settled in. The girls were asleep in their bedrooms upstairs. There were six, so there was no need for them to share. Still, most mornings he woke to find them in his bed, or curled up together in one of their beds.

He wandered into the formal living room, which was nearly empty. He'd bought new furniture for the family room, but Brandon had no idea what he would do with this enormous space.

"Hey," Sara said from behind him.

"Got any bright ideas for this room?" he asked, hands on his hips.

His sister mirrored his stance and looked around. "You could turn it into a game room."

Brandon shook his head. "There's already a game room. And a home theater. And another bonus room." The house had over 6,000 square feet.

Sara's dark brown eyes stared back at him. "Well, I sure can't complain about my rooms. They're really an apartment," she said with a smile. She had a large bedroom, a sitting room, a kitchenette, and full bath on the main floor. "I think they were meant as servants' quarters, but don't get any bright ideas," she added.

Brandon walked over and gave her shoulders a squeeze. "I know, Peanut," he said, using the name he and Landon had tagged her with twenty years ago when she was born. Sara was a foot shorter than him. "You're here to take care of April and Shelbie, nothing more." He gave her a mock grimace. "Certainly not to cook."

"I know," she said with a laugh. "But maybe even I could turn out an edible meal in that kitchen."

The kitchen was a chef's dream. Brandon enjoyed cooking, but never really had the time. Darla had loved to cook and bake. A familiar pain flared in his heart. He wished that he'd been able to give her this kitchen.

He and Sara wandered back into the kitchen. Brandon pulled up a stool to the counter, and Sara got a pitcher of iced tea out of the fridge. "Want some?"

"Sure."

"So, how's the new job? How many famous athletes have you met?" Sara's long blond ponytail swayed behind her.

Brandon laughed. "A couple of Blackhawks' players you probably wouldn't recognize."

She made a face. "Yeah, I don't follow hockey." Brandon fiddled with his phone, brought up a picture of him with the two players, and held it out. Sara cocked an eyebrow. "Maybe I'll start following hockey." She took a swallow. "You got any trips coming up?"

Although it would take him away from his daughters, this was one aspect of his new job that Brandon was really excited about. A doctor always accompanied the team, but as the top orthopedic surgeon at the center, Brandon would have the privilege of going on trips to various championship games, to be on hand to consult and do surgery, just in case. "Yeah, probably with the Cubs this week if they make the playoffs," he said.

"Do you get to ride on a private jet?"

He nodded and smiled. "Sometimes."

"Cool," Sara said.

They sat in silence for a moment. "Sara, I really do appreciate this," Brandon said. "Most sisters wouldn't take a year off college to care for their brother's children."

She shrugged. "It was good timing for me, too." Sara had been studying music at the University of Michigan. "I'm not convinced I was in the right major, and that's an awful lot of money to waste if you don't know what you want. When Mom suggested this, it felt right, and I wanted to help you, too." Her eyes took on a sheen. "I still can't believe Darla's gone. I was so little when you started dating. I don't remember a time when she wasn't there." Sara's voice shook, and a tear escaped and rolled down one cheek. "I still miss her so much."

"Come here," Brandon said, holding out an arm. Sara slipped under it and laid her head on his shoulder. He found himself fighting tears as well. Would the pain ever stop?

"I was closer to her than to my own sister," Sara whispered.

Reagan was almost two years older than Landon, and then Brandon came along less than a year later. Jim and Janice St. Clair thought their family was complete, but God had other ideas. Sara came as a total, although joyful surprise when their children were in their teens. By the time Sara was three, Reagan was off to college, and never lived at home again. And in recent years, the further she climbed up the career ladder, the more holidays she missed.

Sara sniffed and swiped a hand across her cheeks. "I'm going to bed," she said.

"It's only 8:45," Brandon said. "You wanna watch a movie in the home theater?"

Sara shook her head. "Maybe tomorrow night. I'm tired." She kissed her brother's cheek. "'Night."

"Good night, Peanut," Brandon said softly. He looked around and finished the last of his tea. He didn't feel like watching a movie, either. He picked up his phone, pushed a button, and soon his brother's face appeared on the screen.

"Hey, man," Brandon said.

"Right back atcha," Landon replied.

"Is this a good time?"

"Yeah. Babies are down, and I was just finishing up some stuff. What's up?"

Brandon stood. "You want a tour of a multi-million-dollar house?"

Landon laughed. "Heck, yeah. One of my partners has a house like that, but it's not brand new."

Brandon gave him the kitchen tour, and decided to skip Sara's apartment. "Peanut's room is down that hall," he said, "but she already went to bed."

"Before nine?" Landon looked surprised.

Brandon shrugged. "She was tired."

"Hold on." Landon was walking now, too. He opened a door. "Everybody decent?" he called out.

Brandon could tell exactly where he was. "Hi, Kelsea," he called out.

"Oh, hi, Brandon." She laughed. "Yes, I'm in slob mode, but I'm decent." She was propped up in bed, reading.

Landon lay down next to her and adjusted the screen. "We're going on a tour of a million-dollar house," he said "Go back to the kitchen, bro."

"Ooh, awesome!" Kelsea closed her book.

Brandon walked through the house, pointing out all the amenities. He skipped the girls' rooms since they were asleep. Kelsea and Landon thought it was a spectacular home, and agreed with Brandon that there was a lot of space to fill.

"You know, Brandon, Morgan has all kinds of contacts with decorators and artsy people. You really need to call her," Kelsea said.

"Um, yeah, I'll try to do that," he said.

"Do you have her number? I can text it to you."

"Yeah, I'm pretty sure I do." He changed the subject quickly. "Well, guys, I need to do some stuff to get ready for the week. Talk to you soon."

After they'd signed off, Brandon went up to his room. When he turned on the light, the sight of his and Darla's bed sent a fresh wave of pain washing over him. The large dresser looked barren without her things on it. He could see into the enormous walk-in closet that was about a third full of his clothes, but otherwise empty. He was beginning to wonder if this was too much house for them.

Brandon sat down on the bed and sighed, rubbing his eyes. He'd almost sold the bedroom furniture when he left Minneapolis. After all, he was trying to make a fresh start. But in the end, he simply couldn't part with it. He remembered the day that he and Darla had picked it out together.

And how they'd celebrated the first night after it had been delivered.

Brandon stripped to his shorts and t-shirt and tumbled into bed. But it was a long time before sleep found him.

14

MORGAN RACED UP the steps and into her assigned classroom. She still had lots of prep to do before that afternoon's class. She'd overslept this morning—only by ten minutes—but had been playing catch-up all day long.

Her fall semester was fuller than she'd like. Morgan had a heavy teaching and advising load, and she was preparing an article for publication, plus she had her private patients.

She opened her e-mail and scanned them to make sure there wasn't anything there that couldn't wait until tonight to answer. Then Morgan's breath caught. There was an e-mail from Joyce Sheldon, the woman she'd recently talked to about what was needed to begin looking into fostering a child. Morgan had done some more research and thought maybe this would be a better way to go for now.

She quickly read through Joyce's e-mail, and her heart dropped. *So many steps to go through, so much red tape.* She would have to read it more thoroughly tonight.

Her phone pinged with a text. Morgan picked it up and rolled her eyes. *Not again.* Would her sister never give up?

She read the text: *Hey Morgy! Texted Brandon last night and he still hasn't had a chance to get a hold of you. Why don't you call him at his office?* Kelsea had conveniently provided the number.

Morgan couldn't believe it when Kelsea called her a month ago and told her that Brandon and his girls were moving to Chicago. She brushed off her sister's suggestion about helping him figure out how to decorate his house, and gave her busy schedule as an excuse.

That night, Morgan had pulled up the picture of Brandon holding his nephew and stared at it for a long time. It wasn't the first time she'd looked at it since returning home from the family Mother's Day weekend in St. Louis. *Get a hold of yourself. That isn't the real Brandon St. Clair.*

 Morgan didn't have time for distractions today. She had two classes to teach, three patients to see, and finally, a group session to observe conducted by one of her doctoral students. It would be a late night. And as soon as she got home, she would delete that picture from her computer.

Morgan thought tenderly about April and Shelbie. She would love to see them, but had no desire to even talk with their father. Chicago was a big enough city. Millions of people lived here, and with any luck, hers and Dr. St. Clair's paths would never cross.

15

BRANDON SAT AT his desk, answering e-mails. He'd been in his new position for almost a month and was settling in nicely. So far, he loved the job. He'd been on one trip and done five surgeries, all on top-tier athletes with household names. Besides that, he also managed the sports medicine clinic day-to-day, and did a lot of high-level work. He had directives from the board and was working on long-range planning and strategic initiatives. The work challenged him in a way that was different than just performing surgery, and he loved it.

Although Brandon wasn't convinced he liked the suburbs, he was getting used to the house and the neighborhood. He hadn't met any of the neighbors yet, but his sister had. Sara took the girls to the neighborhood park and arranged play dates with (in most cases) the nannies of their little friends. She had enrolled the girls in dance lessons, and as expected, April was taking more to ballet than tap dance, and Shelbie vice versa. They went to activities at the library and even though Sara couldn't boil water, no one was going hungry. The girls adored their Aunt Sara.

Landon had asked him a couple of times if he had found a church home yet, and Brandon kept fudging on that. Although his pain over losing Darla had lessened a bit, and even though he prayed occasionally, he still wasn't on good terms with God and hadn't decided yet what he was going to do.

Brandon got up and took his coffee mug for a refill. When he passed his assistant's desk on the way back, she waved at him. "Oh, hold on. He's here now," she said into the phone.

"Who is it, Giselle?" he asked softly.

She pushed a button that he assumed put the call on hold. "Morgan Anderson," the middle-aged brunette replied.

Oh, no. "Ah—I'll have to call her back," he said. "Just take a message." He went into his office and closed the door.

He walked over to the bank of windows that overlooked Lake Michigan and stared out, nursing his cup of coffee. What was it about Morgan that troubled him so?

His intercom beeped. "Brandon," Giselle said, "they want you down in the clinic. JoJo Collins just arrived." JoJo was one of the NFL's premier players that the Bears had acquired from Denver in the off season. He had a knee that was beginning to act up.

Brandon set his mug down and grabbed his stethoscope. "On my way," he said. Any thoughts about Morgan Anderson would have to wait.

16

TWO DAYS LATER, Brandon played his voicemail messages at the office. "Dr. St. Clair, this is Morgan Anderson." Brandon sat up. Her voice was crisp and businesslike. "My sister tells me that you've moved to Chicago and bought a home. She's decided that you need my help finding someone to help you decorate it, or at least get things up on the walls. You may know that when Kelsea gets an idea in her head, she doesn't let it go. She keeps asking if you've called me, or if I've called you. Now I can tell her that I have. Goodbye."

Brandon listened to the last remaining message and then replayed Morgan's. There sure wasn't any warmth in her voice.

Well, what did you expect? A ticker-tape parade welcoming you to town?

Brandon sighed. Last Sunday, Sara had convinced him to come with her and the girls to church. Although Brandon felt uncomfortable at first, somehow something crept past the walls he'd erected in his heart. The music, the prayers, and even the sermon were a soothing balm to his soul. Maybe he was turning a corner.

He propped a hip on one corner of his desk and stared out the window. *I don't want to do this.* He sat there for another moment.

You're a better man than that. You need to apologize. It's time.

Brandon sighed. He knew when God was talking to him. He used to listen for God's voice regularly, but had gotten out of the habit. Yes, it was time.

He punched the numbers into his phone and as it began ringing, his heart pounded.

"This is Morgan Anderson," her voice said pleasantly.

"Ah—hello, Morgan. This is Brandon St. Clair."

There was a beat of silence. "Yes?" Her voice had turned brittle.

"Well, um, hi. I thought I would return your call. I've been really busy."

"I'm sure you have." Silence yawned between them.

Brandon squirmed. "I, um—well, yeah. I—look. We got off on the wrong foot at Landon and Kelsea's. I—I was just—" He stopped, unable to get the words out.

"Yes?" she prompted.

Man, she's not making this easy.

His conscience pricked at him. *You think you deserve to get off easy?*

Brandon stood, walked over to the windows, and planted his feet in a wide stance. "I behaved badly, Morgan. There's no excuse, but I was overworked, and tired, and I—it was a very rough year." He swallowed. "Please, would you accept my apology? It would—it would mean a lot to me."

There was silence on the other end of the line for a few seconds, and Brandon held his breath. Finally, she spoke. "I—yes, I suppose. And I said some things that I shouldn't have, too. I'm sorry."

He let out a heavy breath. "Wow, I, uh, I feel so much better." *I probably shouldn't have said that.*

To his surprise, she laughed softly. "Me, too."

They chatted for a few moments—mostly about their common niece and nephew and then April and Shelbie—haltingly at first, and then more comfortably.

"So, hey—would you like to see the house?" Brandon heard himself ask. "I'm not asking for your professional opinion or anything. Just come. The girls would love to see you. We're going to grill burgers on Sunday afternoon. About four?"

She didn't say anything. And Brandon had no idea why he had extended the invitation. He swallowed. "Morgan?"

"Sure, yes, that would be fine. Can I bring anything?"

"Oh, no. It will be very informal. Just, um, bring yourself. And there'll be someone special there who I want you to meet."

"Sounds good, Brandon. Well, thank you. Oh—could you text me the address?"

"Will do. See you Sunday, Morgan."

"See you then."

17

MORGAN LOOKED AT the clock again. Had it moved since she'd looked at it last? She checked her phone. Time was crawling by, but it was moving. She couldn't leave yet, or she would arrive way early and appear too anxious.

She checked herself in the mirror again. Should she wear the green top instead? No, she'd already changed twice. *You look fine.*

Morgan grabbed an eyebrow pencil and held her breath as she made one more adjustment. *Why are you so concerned about looking perfect?* she scolded herself. *This isn't a date. You're going to see the girls...and Brandon's just being nice. We're practically family. He hasn't done one thing to indicate that he's interested in you.*

And what if he was? Morgan didn't have the answer to that. Other than the fact that he was outrageously handsome, and seemed to be a good parent, he hadn't demonstrated any redeeming qualities to make Morgan think that he was worthy of her attention.

She puttered around in her kitchen until it was time to

leave. She knew the area where the address was. A couple of years ago, she'd gone to a home not too far from it for a private art showing. Her phone gave clear directions and she made good time.

Morgan turned left onto Evergreen Place. It should be on the right...she passed one palatial home after another. *Wow.* This was some neighborhood. There it was, 48. She pulled into the wide, custom brick driveway and parked behind Brandon's SUV, which now had Illinois plates. A compact car with Wisconsin plates sat next to it. Morgan shook her head to herself. If the cars were in the driveway, what was in the four-car garage?

The house was enormous, all brick and glass. The yard looked new and fresh, and was clearly professionally landscaped, as were all the homes in the neighborhood. She wondered if Brandon had a gardener. This new job of his must be really something.

She rang the doorbell and waited. When the door opened, Morgan was shocked to see a beautiful, petite woman in jeans and a pink v-neck top. Her wavy blond hair was caught up with a glittering clip, and reached halfway to her waist. She had sparkling dark brown eyes and dimples. "Hi, I'm Sara St. Clair," she said. "You must be Morgan. Welcome!"

Morgan's heart dropped. This must be the "someone special" that Brandon had wanted her to meet. *He was married!* Maybe that's why he had moved to Chicago. Kelsea hadn't said anything about that. She glanced at the woman's—correction, *young* woman's left hand, but it was wrapped around the door in such a way that Morgan couldn't see whether or not she wore a ring.

"Yes—yes, I'm Morgan, nice to meet you," she said.

Goodness, but this was awkward. Sara had to be a decade younger than Brandon! His first wife had only been gone a little over a year, and he'd been so devastated just a few months ago. Apparently, he'd gotten past that and moved on.

Morgan knew she couldn't turn and run away, so she stepped into the house. This was a terrible idea. She would make some excuse and get out as quickly as she could.

She took in the two-story entryway and tried not to gawk. It was easily bigger than her entire living room. Sunlight streamed in the multiple windows, throwing rainbows off the gorgeous crystal chandelier hanging overhead. A curved staircase graced the room.

"Miss Morgy!" April and Shelbie cried as they ran up behind Sara. Both of them came right to Morgan and held their arms out, and she leaned down to hug them.

"It's wonderful to see you, girls!" Morgan said.

Shelbie hopped up and down. "You hafta see my room!" she exclaimed. "It's purple!"

Morgan laughed. "I could have guessed that." She turned to April. "What color is your room?"

April smiled shyly. "It's pink and green, like a garden."

"Ooh, I'll bet it's pretty," Morgan said.

"Go ahead, girls, take Morgan upstairs." Sara looked at her. "I'll go check with Brandon and see how the burgers are coming." She glided away.

Morgan set her purse down, and April and Shelbie each took a hand. She spent the next ten minutes with them looking at their pretty bedrooms and meeting their dolls and stuffed animals. When they were finished, they walked down the hall. Shelbie skipped ahead of Morgan and April. "Wanna see Daddy's room?" Shelbie asked.

"Girls?" Brandon's voice floated up from below. "Come on downstairs."

Just in time. They reached the top of the stairs, and as Brandon looked up, his face broke into a smile. He wore cargo shorts, sandals, and a close-fitting navy t-shirt. He looked tanned and fit, and completely at ease. "Hi, Morgan. I see you got the tour."

Morgan's heart fluttered in her chest. *Wow, he's more handsome than ever now that he's relaxed and in his own home and...married.* She immediately felt like she had been doused with cold water.

She managed a smile as she followed the girls down the stairs. "I just saw their rooms." The girls ran ahead, and into what Morgan assumed was the kitchen. She stopped on the bottom stair, which put her even with Brandon. Morgan tucked a wayward strand of hair behind her ear and looked around. Anything to keep her eyes off him. "This is a beautiful home."

"Thanks. It's sure different than anywhere else I've lived." He lifted a shoulder. "I'm beginning to wonder if it's too big. And it's farther from the city than I'd like."

"I live in the city," she said. "I wish I could go to the country."

Brandon made a face. "Not me. I'm a city boy, through and through." He looked at her and smiled. "I'm glad you came. You look great." *He had the most beautiful eyes.*

Morgan felt her face heating up. "Oh, um, thanks." She could hardly breathe in his presence, and becoming infatuated with a married man broke all kinds of rules for her. She scooted around him and stepped off the stair. He turned to her, and she looked away again. "Listen, I'm so sorry, but I'm not going to be able to stay. Something unexpected came up." *That was certainly the truth.*

Brandon's face fell, and Morgan felt terrible. But she had to get out of here. She picked up her purse.

"Morgan, are you sure? The burgers are ready and the girls are so excited—"

Her stomach clenched. *April and Shelbie.* Morgan felt terrible for disappointing them, but she knew she couldn't get through a meal with Brandon and Sara. Morgan reached for the door handle. "Please tell them I'm sorry, and that I promise to come another time and make it up to them." She glanced around to avoid meeting his eyes. "Your home is beautiful. I'll text you some names of some decorators you can contact. Goodbye, Brandon." She slipped out the door as quickly as she dared, made a dash for her car, and drove away without a backward glance.

18

BRANDON STOOD IN the foyer with his hands on his hips. He scratched his head. *What was that all about?* Morgan was here one moment, and gone the next. He had a feeling he was missing something.

Sara came in. "Dinner's almost ready." She looked around. "Where's Morgan? Using the bathroom?"

Brandon shook his head slowly. "No…she left." Her scent still lingered and he was filled with all kinds of conflicting emotions.

"Left? Why?"

"I have no idea. She all of a sudden said that something came up, and she had to go. Something happened, I'm sure of it." He tilted his head at Sara. "Did you say something to her?"

"What, me? No! I just introduced myself and the girls came in and took her up to show her their rooms." She tilted her head back at him. "Maybe *you* said something to her?"

He replayed their very short conversation in his mind, and was more perplexed than ever. "No, I didn't."

Shelbie skipped into the room. "Miss Morgy!" She stopped and looked around. "Where's Miss Morgy?"

"She had to leave, sweetie," Brandon said. He looked at Sara.

"Why she leave?" Shelbie wailed.

Brandon ushered his small daughter toward the kitchen. "Let's eat," he said. He looked over his shoulder at his sister. "I'll figure this out later."

The food was delicious, but Brandon hardly tasted it. The girls were cranky, and he snapped at them once and had to apologize.

"We've had a busy weekend," Sara said. "Girls, let's get upstairs for baths." She looked at Brandon. "Do you want to go with them, or clean this up?"

"I'll do this," he said. He was still distracted, disturbed by Morgan's quick, unexplained exit. He texted Landon. *Hey, has Morgan texted Kelsea tonight?*

His brother answered quickly. *I don't know. Why?*

Brandon didn't feel like explaining. *Never mind. It doesn't matter.*

What's up, bro?

It doesn't matter. Thanks. Gotta go.

Brandon got the leftovers into the fridge and the dishwasher loaded. He looked at his calendar and began preparing his mind for the work week. Then he set some reminders on his schedule for tomorrow and went upstairs to read to the girls and tuck them into bed. Sara said goodnight and went downstairs.

After he said prayers with the girls and turned off the lights, he went into his bedroom to make sure his clothes were ready for morning. Sara had helped him choose a new comforter and linens, and the room didn't have the devastating effect on him that it once had.

He continued to think about Morgan as he put his laundry away. It occurred to him that he was very disappointed that she hadn't stayed, and he didn't know what to make of that. He thought about how pretty she looked, in white cropped pants and royal blue sandals that matched her top, and a long, flowing scarf in shades of blue, yellow, and green. Her long, golden hair had been piled casually on top of her head with pieces of it hanging down to frame her face. Her gorgeous green eyes were perfectly made up in a way that somehow made them stand out. They were absolutely mesmerizing.

Brandon sat down on the edge of the bed. *I think I'm attracted to her.* The thought both thrilled and scared him. He hadn't given any woman a second glance in the almost year and a half that he'd been a widower.

He headed downstairs and had just stepped off the bottom stair when his phone pinged. It was Landon.

Sara introduced herself to Morgan as Sara St. Clair.

So what? Brandon thought. He responded, *It's her name. How else would she introduce herself?*

She never said she was your sister. Think about it, man. Put yourself in Morgan's shoes.

"Oh, no…" Brandon finally understood. He sat down on the bottom stair. *I got it, thanks,* he typed, and signed off. He sat there for a long time, deep in thought, and finally, a slow smile spread across his face.

19

MORGAN GATHERED UP her things to get ready to leave work. It had been a long day, a long week already, and it was only Wednesday. She and Joyce Sheldon had exchanged a few e-mails. Morgan had more questions than ever, and was starting to think that fostering was the way to go. She had asked Joyce to send her the necessary paperwork to prepare her application, but hadn't heard anything back yet.

Maybe she would get out of town this weekend, go to the country and paint. Morgan's good friends, Luke and Miranda, lived on a large farm west of Chicago. There was a secluded, rustic cabin on their property overlooking a beautiful pond, and Morgan had an open invitation anytime she wanted to come. *Yes, I'll go,* she decided. She needed to clear her head of Brandon St. Clair and decide if she was ready to move forward and bring a child into her life.

The first thing Morgan had done when she arrived home from Brandon's house on Sunday evening was to delete the picture of him from her computer. Then she immediately texted her sister. Morgan didn't want to admit that she'd run away from Brandon's house, so she skipped that part. *I met Brandon's wife* was all she had said. Of course, Kelsea called her right away, and they sorted the whole thing out. Morgan tried to be upbeat and laugh it off, but she was absolutely mortified at her misassumption. In the three years that she'd known her brother-in-law, she had only heard him refer to his younger sister as *Peanut*. Morgan begged Kelsea not to tell Landon, but by then he had heard his wife's end of the conversation and knew something was going on, so of course they had to share the whole story with him.

Morgan knew it would eventually get back to Brandon, and she could never look him in the eye again. Or Sara.

Morgan didn't fall asleep for a long time that night. She thought about retrieving the deleted photo and decided to leave it be. The thing that haunted her the most was that she seemed to be attracted to Brandon St. Clair, and that terrified her. Morgan didn't have a lot of experience with men. She didn't date in high school because she was so busy taking AP classes and designing sets for the drama club, and spending all her nights and weekends in art galleries and at art shows. College was more of the same, with a few occasional dates. Getting her PhD before she turned thirty left little time for romance or anything else, and she'd never really met a guy that challenged her intellectually or who interested her.

Until Patrick. But she wasn't going to think about him.

Maybe, just maybe, Brandon was a little interested too, and that's why he had invited her to his house. And then she completely blew it. But maybe he was just being nice, and wasn't even interested. Morgan had no idea how these male/female games worked.

Brandon had almost completely filled her thoughts since Sunday night. And then, as if she had the power to conjure him up just by thinking about him, he appeared in the doorway of her office, holding a large bouquet of calla lilies.

Morgan was standing at the round meeting table in her office, sorting through some papers, and almost dropped the pile of folders that she was holding. Heaven help her, he was unbelievably handsome in a navy suit, crisp white shirt, and a blue patterned tie. Her entire body went cold, then hot, and her knees turned to jelly. Morgan felt her face flaming. She could hardly make eye contact with him.

"Hi," he said with a smile.

This cannot be happening. A thousand thoughts collided inside Morgan's mind. First, of course, was that he'd talked with Kelsea and Landon. Otherwise, how did he know that her favorite flowers in the whole world were calla lilies? She wished the floor would swallow her up.

"Hi," she tried to say back, but hardly any sound came out.

He stepped into her office and tipped his head toward the door. "Mind if I close this?"

Morgan shook her head. He shut the door and suddenly, the room felt half its normal size.

Brandon walked over to her. "Let's sit down," he said, gently taking her elbow. She must have looked on the verge of fainting. Morgan sank into one of the chairs at the round table. He laid the flowers down and pulled up a chair next to her.

She felt like she could burst into tears at any moment. She swallowed. "Brandon, I'm so embarrassed—"

"Shh," he whispered. "You don't have anything to be

embarrassed about, or to be sorry for." His amber gaze held hers for a moment. "Are you seeing anyone right now?"

Surely he can't mean… "Am I seeing anyone?" she heard herself say. No way was she going to answer him for fear of making another misassumption.

"What I meant to say was, are you dating anyone?"

"Am I dating anyone?"

He nodded.

She shook her head.

"Would you go out with me?"

Morgan thought she must be hearing things. "Would I go out with you?"

Brandon glanced around. "Is there an echo in here?" he said with a smile. "Yes. I want to take you out, on a date."

"On a date?"

He laughed, and Morgan almost melted into a puddle at his handsomeness. She wanted to pinch herself. She had to be dreaming. "I don't understand."

Brandon scratched his chin. "When I invited you over last Sunday, I wasn't thinking anything. I guess I just figured that it would be an extra goodwill gesture to apologize for how badly I acted toward you when we first met."

He took a breath, reached out, and wrapped his hand around hers. Morgan swore a jolt of electricity shot clear down to her toes. "But when you left, I was so disappointed, and that surprised me. I did a lot of thinking that night, and realized that I was attracted to you, and that I was looking forward to getting to know you better."

Morgan's heart began to pound. She looked down at Brandon's long, smooth fingers holding hers, and she gazed into his eyes again. *His incredible golden amber eyes.* They took on a twinkle. "And then, when I found out why you had left so suddenly, I realized that if you weren't interested in me, you wouldn't care whether or not I was married." His smile got bigger. "Am I right?"

Something in Morgan's heart burst, and she felt liquid joy running through her veins. She couldn't believe that Brandon St. Clair was sitting here, holding her hand and telling her that he was attracted to her and wanted to date her.

It gave her confidence to not hold back. She nodded. "Yes. You were right."

He let out a breath. "Oh, good," he said, and they both laughed.

"Sara doesn't look anything like me," he explained. "She's blond like Landon, but he and I look alike. Our older sister Reagan has dark hair like mine, but she looks like Sara." He grinned. "Does that make sense?"

Morgan nodded. "Yeah, it does. Kelsea and I don't really look alike. She resembles our mom, and I look like our dad." She felt a surge of boldness. "I can't believe this is happening," she said. She felt like her smile might split her face open.

"Me, too," Brandon said. His eyes sparkled. He let go of her hand and picked up the bouquet and held it out.

"I love calla lilies, thank you." She slid him a mischievous look. "How did you know that they're my favorites?"

"Kelsea may have told me."

"I figured," Morgan replied with a giggle. She couldn't remember the last time she had giggled.

Brandon leaned forward and rested his arms on the table.

"Let's figure this out together. I'm close to Landon, and you're close to Kelsea. What's your comfort level with what we each tell them?"

Morgan thought for a moment. "I think I'd like to keep things to ourselves until we figure out things out a little more," she said.

"That's exactly what I was thinking. For now, it will be our secret." He smiled, and Morgan's stomach did a flip. He took her hand again. "I've talked with them, and the misunderstanding about Sara will stay with the four of us, and we'll never mention it again. Do you understand what I'm saying?"

Morgan let out a breath of relief. "Yes. Thank you, Brandon."

"Sara will never know, unless you choose to tell her. Okay?"

She nodded. He stood and helped Morgan to her feet. "I think I owe you a dinner."

Morgan laughed. "I'm the one who ran out. I owe *you* a dinner."

His eyebrows lifted. "Are you free tonight?"

"I could be persuaded."

"In that case…" He leaned down and brushed his lips across hers. Morgan thought she might faint. "Do you need some more persuading?" he whispered. His eyes sparkled.

Morgan held her breath. *I'll never get another chance like this.* Then she nodded, and everything went into slow motion. As he came closer, his amber eyes darkened a shade, and once Morgan closed her own eyes, her other senses took over. The feel of his soft, firm lips on hers, and the solidness of his shoulders as she ran her hands up and over them. His unique, masculine scent. The sound of her sigh as his arms pulled her close, and of his soft answering moan. The taste of his mouth intermingled with hers.

When they finally came apart, he just held her, for which she was grateful. She was definitely experiencing sensory overload.

If Brandon St. Clair kissed her a million more times— and Morgan sincerely hoped that would be the case—she would still remember *this* kiss for the rest of her life.

20

GO BIG OR go home. That was his and Landon's mantra in everything they attempted. The St. Clair brothers had always set big goals in their professional and personal lives, and it was the reason Brandon had been able to so boldly state his intentions to Morgan tonight. And, for heaven's sake, to kiss her before the date even began. He'd never done anything like that before. But he couldn't keep his eyes off her rosy lips, and almost before he realized what he was doing, he was kissing her.

That second kiss was really something. Brandon was overwhelmed by her feminine softness, and the way she fit in his arms. Almost before he could wonder if he was moving too quickly, he realized that she was as eager a participant as he. They were both breathless when they came apart.

Once Brandon had figured out that he was attracted to Morgan and that she certainly must feel the same way, he set his course for full-steam ahead. Darla was the only woman he had ever dated, and they had met when they were seventeen. Brandon had no patience for dating games, or any knowledge of how they worked.

He and Morgan were sitting in his SUV now. She wore a long, flowing skirt with a swirling pattern in vibrant blues, greens, and purples, and a blue gauzy blouse. The total effect brought out the green in her eyes, and Brandon could hardly keep from staring at her.

"You're the one who knows this city," he said. "Where should we eat?"

"Gosh, there are so many good restaurants," Morgan replied. "What are you in the mood for?"

Brandon's mind went to a place that it had no business going on a first date. He dragged his gaze from her and shifted in his seat. "I'll eat just about anything." He looked out the window. "It's a beautiful fall evening. Maybe somewhere with a patio?"

"Oh, my gosh!" Morgan exclaimed, causing him to jump. "Autumn Evening!" When Brandon didn't say anything, she smiled. "It's a restaurant, and it has a patio. It's perfect."

They got there in under twenty minutes, and it *was* perfect. It might have been the most perfect evening in Brandon's life, or at least in a very long time. After they were seated on the patio and the server brought glasses of water, Brandon studied the menu and was surprised when he heard Morgan say, "What looks good to you?"

You, he instantly thought. He felt his face flush, and took a long drink of his water. He couldn't remember anything that he'd just read. "I—wow," he gulped. "To tell you the truth, my stomach is so jittery, I don't think I can eat much."

Morgan laughed and gave him a dazzling smile. "Me, too." She tucked a strand of hair behind her ear in what seemed like a nervous gesture. Brandon wanted to grab her hand and kiss it.

"Would you want to split an entrée?" he asked, and she nodded and looked relieved. They ended up each ordering a salad and sharing an order of fettucine Alfredo, and later, a piece of raspberry cheesecake.

He wanted to know everything about her. She'd grown up in Kankakee, Illinois with her mom, dad, and of course, her older sister. Their dad died of a heart attack when Morgan was ten and Kelsea was twelve. Brandon held her hand as she talked about that period in her life, and how art filled the deep fissures of her soul and helped set the course for her life's work.

"I know you think art therapy is silly," she said.

Brandon held up a hand. "Don't hold me responsible for anything I said the weekend we met," he said. "Although, I really don't understand it." He smiled. "But I'm willing to try."

"How's April doing?" Morgan asked.

Brandon let out a deep breath and shook his head. "Some things are better since Pea—Sara—is here with us and keeps the girls on a schedule, but April still wakes up crying during the night, and sometimes she disappears during the day and we find her curled up on her bed."

"I'm sorry," Morgan said softly. "I was older when I lost my dad, and it took me a long time to work through it. Something like that changes you forever."

Brandon nodded. "I would give *anything* in the world for my girls to not have to go through this," he said softly. He felt his eyes tearing up and was surprised when he felt Morgan's soft, smooth hand on his. She didn't say anything, but he felt immensely comforted by her touch.

They had coffee with their dessert, and stayed long after

everyone else had left, holding hands almost the entire time. He couldn't keep his eyes off her long, graceful fingers. Brandon felt like they were in a private, romantic universe of their own, with hundreds of twinkling lights on the fence and in the trees around them, and the cool, calm breeze playing with Morgan's luxurious, sun-streaked hair. He itched to run his fingers through it.

Their server finally appeared, an apologetic look on his face. "We're getting ready to close," he said. Brandon signed the check with a generous tip, and they left.

He laced his fingers with Morgan's and they walked slowly to the car. When they got there, he turned and laid his hands on her shoulders. "This was a perfect evening," he whispered. "Thank you for going out with me."

"Thank you for asking," she said, and lifted her face to his. Brandon explored her lips and savored the tastes of raspberry and coffee. Then he looked into her gorgeous green eyes and rubbed his hands up and down her arms. "I—it's so amazing to hold you," he said. "You're so tall, and so close." He swallowed. "Darla was really short." Then he realized what he was saying, and his breath caught. "Morgan, I'm so sorry—"

She shook her head and raised one graceful hand to touch the side of his face. "Don't be, Bran. It's okay. She was part of you."

"I—wow." Brandon pulled her a little closer and smiled. "Bran? I like that. No one has ever called me that."

Morgan smiled. "It fits."

"Where's your car?" he asked. Brandon wished he could take her home.

"I took the El to work. There's a station a block away."

Perfect. Brandon tilted his head at her and smiled. "You are *crazy* if you think I'm going to let you take the El home." He unlocked the passenger door and helped her in.

It was about a twenty-minute drive to her condo, and felt like two. They found so many things to laugh and talk about. Brandon felt like a teenager when he walked Morgan to her doorstep and took her in his arms.

"Can you come for dinner Friday night?" he said. "The girls will be so excited."

"I'd love to. What about Sara?"

"You mean, should we tell her?" Brandon chuckled. "Not yet, unless you want to hear about it on CNN. She can't keep a secret."

Morgan's laughter was like music to him.

"We'll sneak off for kisses," he said huskily.

"Then I'll definitely come. Text me when you get home?" Morgan asked.

"I live way out in the 'burbs," he said. "It'll take me a while. Will you still be up?"

Her eyes sparkled at him under the porch light. "I don't think I'll be able to fall asleep anytime soon."

He laughed and touched his forehead to hers. "I understand. Completely." Then he kissed her, slow and sweet, holding himself to one kiss. "Goodnight, Morgan." He waited until she'd gotten inside and locked the door.

Brandon replayed every moment of their date on the way home, and couldn't stop smiling. Forty minutes later, he pulled into his garage and sent her a text. *Made it home. Sweet dreams.*

They sure will be ☺, she replied.

21

"DR. ANDERSON?"

Morgan snapped back to the present. She'd been staring at her phone screen, which now held the picture of Brandon with Isaac that she'd been able to recover from her computer last night. She'd looked at it at least a thousand times today.

One of her most promising master's students, Lexi Montgomery, stood in her office doorway. "Oh, I'm sorry—hi, Lexi," she said. "Come on in."

She spent the next fifteen minutes with Lexi, who laid out her plans for a very promising research project. Another student came after that, and then Morgan got through all her e-mails and answered them. Before she knew it, her office hours were over.

She felt like she'd been in a dream since last night. *Was it just last night?* Morgan looked at the time. It'd been less than twenty-four hours. She touched her fingers to her lips. *That kiss.* Not the first one—although she'd felt that one clear down to her toes—but the second one, in her office.

Morgan felt that one in every part of her body. She'd never been kissed like that before. And she couldn't believe that she'd kissed him back.

And his subsequent kisses were just as powerful.

Morgan had never experienced a man like Brandon St. Clair. He was so bold and confident and commanding. He was really interested in *her?* Quiet, boring, studious Morgan Ashley Anderson?

Her phone pinged an alarm, and she realized it was time for the weekly department faculty meeting. Morgan gathered her things and locked her door behind her.

Her cell rang. "Dr. Anderson," she said as she walked down the hallway.

"Dr. St. Clair," came the suave reply.

Morgan thought she felt her feet come off the floor. "Hi," she said, and grimaced inwardly. Why couldn't she think of something more interesting to say?

"Hi," he answered. Then he laughed. "Now I'm the one echoing *you.*" Morgan joined his laughter. "How's your day going?"

"Great. It's going great," Morgan replied. "What about you?"

"My day is—fantastic," he said. "I can't stop thinking about last night, and I can't stop thinking about how good it feels to hold you."

Morgan stopped dead in her tracks. No man had ever said anything so romantic to her. She had no idea how to reply.

"I'm sorry," Brandon said. "Too much, too soon?"

"What? No, not at all, Bran. I—" she looked around to make sure she was alone. "I had such a great time last night."

"Oh no, I sense a *but* coming," he said softly.

Morgan took another deep breath. "Not at all. What I was going to say was—that I can't stop thinking about you, too, and—" *You can do this.* "I can't wait to kiss you again."

"Wow." He let out a low whistle, and Morgan giggled. Her face felt hot. "You just made my day," he said. His voice had gone a little husky, and Morgan suppressed a shiver.

"You made mine, too, just by calling." She was almost to the conference room. "I'm sorry, I have to go. Faculty meeting. Bleh."

"Sounds like our staff meetings. I'll let you go. I'll call you tonight."

"You'd better," she said with a smile. *Where are these bold words coming from?*

"Bye, Morgan."

"Bye, Bran." Morgan slipped her phone in her pocket and entered the room.

The department chair, Dr. Juanita Ross, looked up. She had been Morgan's mentor all through her master's and doctoral work, and knew her well. "Hi, Morgan," she said. She stared at Morgan for a moment.

"Um—hi, Juanita." Morgan quickly found a seat.

Juanita gave her a quizzical look. "You look—different. Is something going on?"

Breathe. Morgan felt a couple of other colleagues sizing her up.

"You look happy, like really, really happy," Juanita said.

Morgan flipped her hair over her shoulder. "Oh—yes, I'm happy. Um—Lexi Montgomery just came up with a really amazing idea for a research project." She resisted the urge to laugh hysterically. Morgan uncapped her water bottle and took a gulp.

"That's great," Juanita said. She didn't look entirely convinced. She looked around the table. "Well, let's get started."

22

THE HOURS BETWEEN Wednesday night and Friday crawled. Brandon couldn't wait to see Morgan, but he knew he had to act casual and pretend that she was nothing more than a family friend coming over for dinner.

He got home from work and decided to take a shower. When he walked into the kitchen, Sara and the girls were there. "Chicken is ready to go on the grill," she said. He picked up the plate and gathered the other supplies he'd need.

"Whoa," Sara said, and gave an exaggerated wheeze. Brandon stopped. "What did you do, bathe in aftershave?" She raised her eyebrows and smiled.

Oh no. He rolled his eyes. "So I shaved. You're such a drama queen." He hurried out the door.

Brandon forced himself to stay by the grill and let Sara and the girls get the door when Morgan arrived. When April and Shelbie led her out onto the deck, his heart began a crazy dance. She wore a beautiful flowered dress with a full skirt that floated around her legs. It was casual, yet elegant.

"Hi, Morgan," he managed to say calmly. "Glad you came."

"Hi, Brandon, thanks," she said.

Is her heart beating as hard as mine is?

The girls wanted to show her the yard and all their outside toys. April showed great delight in pointing out the fall flowers that the landscaper had planted. The girls monopolized her attention and that was fine with Brandon. He didn't know if he could have a conversation with her and keep his wits about him.

They sat down to eat, and Sara and Morgan chatted easily. Sara was a very talented vocalist and had been majoring in music.

"I made a new friend today," Shelbie announced. Sara had begun taking the girls to a nearby park.

"Oh, who's that?" Brandon asked.

"His name is AJ. I like the name AJ. I want our little brother's name to be AJ."

"Me, too," said April.

Oh, no. Brandon forced himself not to cringe. Why wouldn't the girls drop this obsession about having a little brother? "Who can eat ten peas first? Ready, set, go!" Fortunately, the game distracted the girls. When Brandon chanced a glance at Morgan, she was looking down at her plate, and her cheeks were definitely tinged a little pink.

Morgan scooted her chair back. "Could someone point me to the restroom?"

Brandon popped up. "I'll show you where it is." He opened the French doors and ushered her through. Once they were through the kitchen, he grinned and took her hand. His heart was hammering. He led her into the half bath off the large entry foyer, turned on the light, and closed the door. In about a second, she was in his arms. "I've missed you so much, babe," he murmured.

She gazed up at him with a gorgeous smile. "Babe? I like that. No one has ever called me babe."

He locked his arms behind her waist. "I've never called anyone that. It fits." He bent his head to kiss her, and they spent a few more moments smiling and whispering about absolutely nothing. It was enough for Brandon just to hold her. "I should get back. Wait a few minutes and then come back out."

Morgan nodded and giggled. "Sneaking away to a bathroom. This is so romantic."

Brandon laughed. "I couldn't wait one more minute to kiss you." He put his hands on her shoulders. "Could I come to your place for a while tonight, later? I'll tell Sara I have to go check on something at the Center."

Morgan's emerald eyes sparkled. "I'd like that. Do you remember how to get there?"

Brandon nodded, then hesitated. "Could you do me a favor?" he asked. She nodded. "Even though I'll see you in a little while, *please* call or text me when you're safe at home. I just—I just need to know."

She reached out and squeezed his hand, and Brandon knew that she understood. "I will, I promise."

Brandon touched his lips to hers. "Save me some kisses," he murmured.

"I will."

Brandon willed his heart to beat normally and hurried back to the patio, slowing his steps as he arrived. Sara looked at him quizzically. "That took a while."

He sat and took another helping of potato salad. "I heard a noise outside."

"Maybe it was the neighbor's cat," Sara mused.

"It was. That's what it was. The neighbor's cat."

She tilted her head at him. "None of our neighbors have a cat, Brandon."

Brandon ignored her and turned his attention to his daughters. "Tell me about going to the library today, girls."

23

MORGAN KICKED OFF her shoes and laid her purse and keys on the hall table. She turned on some lights and cast a critical eye around her condo. What would Brandon think of it? It was so much smaller than his expansive home.

Morgan was a tidy person and there really wasn't any clutter, but she straightened up some things and checked her coffee pods. She knew Brandon drank coffee and she hoped there would be something there he liked.

Then she ran up to her bedroom, spritzed on her favorite light scent, and swiped on some lip gloss. Morgan stared at herself in the reflection. What was that business about Brandon's girls wanting a little brother? She faintly recalled something about it from last spring at Kelsea and Landon's house.

Morgan sat down on the edge of her bed. What was she going to do? Should she say something to him about her infertility issues? Her head and her heart were at war. *No, it's definitely too soon.*

The doorbell rang, and she scurried back downstairs and

drew in a shaky breath before opening the door, willing the butterflies in her stomach to stop fluttering.

He completely filled the doorframe. "Hi," he said. Brandon's smile reached from ear to ear, and his handsomeness nearly caused her to melt.

"Hi, come in," Morgan said shyly. All of a sudden, she felt—well, she didn't know what she was feeling. They'd been together in her office and a restaurant, and in his car in the parking lot—all public places—and then at his home tonight with Sara and the girls in close proximity. But now they were completely alone.

Morgan was both excited and terrified. She wasn't sure what he expected. She closed the door and turned to face him.

He reached out and took her hand. "What's the matter, Morgan?"

"What's the matter?" she echoed.

Brandon took her other hand and smiled. "When you're nervous, you repeat whatever I say. And it's *adorable.*"

She couldn't help but laugh, and he joined her. "Come here." Brandon wrapped his arms around her, and tucked her head into the space between his shoulder and neck. They stood there like that for several moments, his hand stroking her hair. "I just want to spend some time with you and get to know you better," he said softly.

"Sounds perfect," Morgan replied. She let out a breath. "Would you like some coffee?"

He smiled. "I'd love some," and followed her into the kitchen. Morgan learned his favorite flavor of coffee, and decided that as soon as he left, she'd go online and order a case of it.

When they went back into the living room, Morgan realized that she'd left her laptop open on the coffee table. *Oh, no.*

"Nice screensaver," Brandon commented with a sparkling smile that rivaled the one in the photo.

Morgan set the tray down and wondered how to explain it to him, but he didn't give her the chance. Instead, he pulled her into his arms. "I'm extremely flattered," he whispered, and then captured her lips in a delicious kiss.

They sat down on the couch, and both of them sipped their coffee. "I didn't take that picture of you," Morgan said. "It showed up on my phone after I got home from St. Louis. Do you remember who took it?"

Brandon frowned. "I don't. There were so many phone cameras around all weekend." He pulled his phone out and held it up. Morgan was surprised to see the background was a picture of her with April and Shelbie in Landon and Kelsea's backyard. She remembered they had been looking at a caterpillar. "You took that?" she asked.

He shook his head. "Nope. I found it on my phone after I got home." He fixed her with a long gaze. "I couldn't bring myself to delete it."

Morgan laughed. "I'm extremely flattered," she said softly, and boldly leaned in and kissed him.

"Somebody must have been trying to do some matchmaking that weekend," Brandon said with a grin. Then he asked her about her work, and Morgan lost herself talking about her research interests and her patients. She could tell by his questions that he was sincerely interested.

Suddenly, his watch beeped, and Morgan hoped that he wasn't going to leave. She was surprised when he took her mug from her and set both of them down on the table, then wrapped both arms around her. She looked at him. "What's going on?"

"Kissing break," he said.

She laughed. "You set your watch for a kissing break?"

"Yep. Sixty seconds of kissing, then twenty minutes of talking, then sixty more seconds of kissing." His eyes sparkled and Morgan felt herself drowning in them.

"Oh, Bran," she said, trying not to laugh. "That is so adorable. And so precise."

He leaned in. "No talking during kissing time, babe," he whispered, and pressed his lips to hers.

When his alarm went off again, she sighed. "That went too fast."

He drew back and picked up his mug. "I know, but I also know my limits," he said, and then he winked. That almost undid Morgan. So she asked him to tell her about his new job, and was fascinated by it. She thought of all kinds of questions to ask him.

The time sped by and they went through several cycles of talking and kissing breaks. Then Brandon's watch made a different kind of beep. He sighed. "That means it's time for me to go." Morgan looked at the clock and was shocked to realize that he'd been there for three and a half hours.

She walked him to the door, and they wrapped their arms around one another. "Thank you for coming over," she said. "I had such a wonderful time."

"Me, too," he said. "Can I see you again this weekend?"

Her heart tripped. "Yes! Of course. What did you have in mind?"

"Have you ever been to an NBA game?"

She shook her head.

"How about tomorrow night?"

"I'd love it," Morgan said with a smile.

He smiled back. "Good. The Bulls are in town. I'll come by for you around 6:30. I should be able to get away for a while on Sunday afternoon. We'll figure out something to do."

"Why don't I plan it, since you planned tomorrow night?"

"It's a deal." He kissed her, and Morgan thought this may have been the best night of her life.

Brandon opened the door and stepped out. "Goodnight, babe," he whispered.

"Goodnight, Bran. Text me when you get home?"

"I sure will."

24

IT WAS WEDNESDAY morning, exactly a week after their first date, and Brandon hadn't seen Morgan since Sunday afternoon. Three dates in three days had made it the best weekend he could remember in a long time. It was a good thing they were having dinner tonight, because he didn't think he could go another day without seeing her.

He pulled on his suit jacket, walked into the kitchen, and poured coffee into his travel mug for the commute into work.

Sara was slumped at the kitchen table in her fluffy robe, and had a serious case of bedhead. She glared at him. "What is up with you and this whistling all of a sudden?"

Brandon stopped. He didn't realize he'd been whistling. "You're such a grump in the morning, Peanut."

"That's because I should be sleeping for another four hours," she yawned. April and Shelbie skipped into the room. They were still in their pajamas. "How do they have so much energy at this time of day?" Sara muttered to no one in particular.

Brandon set his things down and opened his arms.

"Come give me hugs, girls." He squatted down and his daughters covered him with hugs and kisses.

"Do you have a meeting tonight, Daddy?" April asked.

"Yes, but it won't be late, I promise. I'll be home in plenty of time for stories and bedtime." He and Morgan had decided that on the nights they could get together, to do an early dinner. Brandon was thankful that her schedule had that kind of flexibility.

Brandon said goodbye to Sara and the girls and climbed into his SUV. He set his phone in its holder on the dash and hit speed dial as he pulled out of the driveway. "Morning, babe," he said when Morgan answered.

"Morning, Bran." They fell into easy conversation. She told him everything she had planned for the day. "Where do you want to have dinner?" she asked.

"Well, it's our one-week anniversary, so it should be special," he replied.

"One week? Wow, you're right," Morgan said. She sounded surprised.

"It feels like a lot longer, doesn't it?" Brandon said.

"Yes, it does."

"I'm enjoying every minute of it," he said.

"Me, too." He could hear the smile in her voice.

"How about Peppito's?"

"Perfect. I haven't been there in a while. See you at five? I'll meet you there. I'll be coming straight from a session."

"You're riding the El today, right?" he asked.

"Yes, why?"

"Because that means I can take you home and get a proper goodnight kiss."

"Count on it," Morgan responded. He could tell she was still smiling.

They said goodbye and Brandon turned his attention to the road. He hadn't even realized he was stuck in traffic. He drummed his fingers on the steering wheel and thought about the last week. *I can't believe it's only been a week.* It was amazing, being with Morgan. Sometimes a spear of guilt would prick him. Was it too soon? Darla had been gone for almost a year and a half. Brandon had been sure that he would never, ever be interested in being with anyone else. And then it just happened.

Am I in love with Morgan? Brandon honestly couldn't answer that. It was way too soon. All he knew was that it felt so good to not be alone, to have someone to fill all the lost and lonely places of his soul. He wanted to join life again, to do all the things he used to enjoy. He wasn't sure how Morgan had liked the Bulls game. She'd spent most of the night with her hands over her ears.

Sunday afternoon, she'd taken him to some art gallery. Brandon was bored out of his mind, but enjoyed the opportunity to hold her hand and watch her lovely features come to life as she explained all kinds of things about the artwork to him.

Brandon arrived at the restaurant first, and waited for Morgan in the lobby. Every time the door opened, his gaze flew to it, and when she finally walked in, he felt his chest swell at her loveliness.

Her hair fell past her shoulders in soft waves, and she was dressed in teal-blue in her typical graceful, flowing style. Then it hit him. This was one of the biggest differences between Morgan and Darla—Morgan was so feminine. Dar was pretty, but clothes, hair, and makeup had never been her priority. She pulled her hair back in a ponytail and pretty much wore scrubs or jeans and a t-shirt 24/7. Once a year she might put on a dress and some makeup for a special occasion. It had never bothered Brandon because that was her style and he loved her, but now with Morgan, the contrast was striking.

Brandon wanted so badly to sweep Morgan into his arms and kiss her senseless, but settled for a quick peck. "Hi, babe," he murmured.

The hostess ushered them to their table, handed them menus, and left. Brandon let out a sigh.

"What's wrong, Bran?" she asked.

He reached for her hand and leaned in close. "Nothing, except that I want to go somewhere and be alone with you and kiss you until neither of us can breathe."

Her face turned pink and she squeezed his hand. "It's probably a good thing that we're in public," she said. "But I'll hold you to that." She smiled and her gaze rested on his lips.

He inhaled sharply, then raised her hand and kissed it. "Not fair," he said with a smile.

She responded with a musical laugh. Brandon's heart skittered in his chest.

They ordered their food and he asked her about her day. Brandon thought they would never get through the meal, but when they got in the car, he looked at the clock and realized that they'd only been in the restaurant for an hour. That gave him plenty of time to get Morgan home and say goodnight to her before he needed to leave for home.

As soon as they got through her front door, he pulled her

into his arms and made good on his promise. When they finally came up for air, he buried his face in her hair and breathed her in. "Mmm…tonight was…wonderful."

Morgan tipped her head back and gazed up at him, and ran her fingertip along his bottom lip. "Better than the art gallery?"

"What? I enjoyed that, too." He grinned at her.

"Liar," she whispered with a smile.

He laughed. Then something occurred to him. "What about the game Saturday night?" He locked his hands behind her waist.

Morgan looked surprised. "Oh, I liked it," she said a little too brightly.

Brandon brushed a kiss on her lips. "Liar," he said. He moved in for a longer, deeper kiss.

When he turned his attention to her neck, Morgan ran her fingers up and through his hair. "Just being with you is enough for me," she whispered. "It doesn't matter where we are or what we're doing."

Brandon's lips found hers again. "Me, too." His watch alarm beeped, and he loosened his hold on her. "I wish I didn't have to go." He touched his forehead to hers.

Morgan put her finger over his lips and shook her head. "April and Shelbie are your priority right now. I wouldn't have it any other way." She cradled his face in her hands and whispered, "you're such a good dad, Bran," and he felt like he could fly.

"I'll call you after the girls are asleep."

"I'll be waiting," she said.

The next week and a half flew by. He ended up making two quick, unscheduled trips, and was up to his neck in work at the Center. She was busy, too, and they managed a few quick lunches and stolen kisses.

One evening when they were at Morgan's condo, they had just finished their takeout meal when a steady, gentle rain began to fall. Morgan grabbed an umbrella and begged Brandon to go for a walk. At first, he protested. Walking was a means by which to get from point A to point B. He and Darla had certainly never done anything like that. Almost from the day they'd met, they were immersed in studying or work, and later, caring for two babies and juggling two high-powered, stressful careers.

But as he and Morgan strolled in the early evening twilight, Brandon began to relax and focus on the sights, sounds, and smells of autumn around them. The rain began to come down a little harder, and he felt like they were in a world of their own under the umbrella. He thoroughly enjoyed holding Morgan close and stopping for an occasional kiss. It was a completely wonderful, romantic experience.

The weekend of Halloween, Sara wanted to go to a movie with some friends, so Brandon invited Morgan over. The cover story was that she was coming to measure some walls. Sara had gotten fairy princess costumes for the girls, and he took them to a few nearby houses while Morgan stayed at the house and passed out candy.

The girls were so excited that "Miss Morgy" was there, and between that and the candy he'd let them eat, it was hard to get them to sleep. But finally, once he was sure they were down for the night, he led Morgan to the family room couch and took her into his arms. She was right; just being together was enough.

Brandon had told Sara to text him when she was on her way home, so he was confident that they'd have enough time for Morgan to get away before Sara arrived.

"What are you doing Sunday?" he said. "We could do something during the afternoon."

Morgan nibbled on her lower lip and looked a little sheepish. "Well, Sunday is my birthday."

"Babe! Really?" Then it occurred to Brandon that they'd never gotten around to little details like that. "What would you like to do? I'll take you out." The Bears were in town that weekend and were the hottest ticket in town. Brandon had a standing invitation for the owner's box. Wouldn't that bowl Morgan over if he took her there? It wouldn't be as fast-paced and noisy as the basketball game. He started to open his mouth, and then her face lit up.

"There's a symphonic wind concert at U of I. I know the conductor and I'm sure we could get tickets. They're doing Vivaldi's *Four Seasons*, one of my favorites."

Brandon had no idea what any of that meant, and he thought it sounded like a horrible way to spend an afternoon, but it was her birthday, so she should be able to choose. He smiled at her. "It's a date," he said.

"So, when is *your* birthday?"

He sighed. "Christmas Eve."

"Really? Poor Bran," she said, sounding sincere.

"Yeah, I always felt gypped growing up. But now it's not so bad, really. It's more or less a holiday, so everyone's around." He gazed into her eyes. "Maybe we can get together on my birthday this year." That was a pretty bold move, to suggest that they might spend Christmas together, but he wanted to see her reaction.

She smiled and rubbed her hands over his shoulders. "Maybe we can," she said a little flirtatiously. "I think we'd have to tell our families that we're dating," she said.

"Yeah," he agreed. "What are you doing for Thanksgiving?"

"I'm not sure. What about you?"

"I think we're all going to my parents' house this year. If Landon and Kelsea and the twins come, I'm sure you and your mom would be welcome."

"That'd be fun," Morgan said. "Will your older sister come from Florida?"

Brandon shook his head. "I doubt it. Reagan's a workaholic. She's not exactly the black sheep of the family, but she's not as close as the rest of us are." He shrugged. "If she comes, it will be last minute, and she'll just blow in like a hurricane."

Morgan laughed. "What does she do?"

"She's an assistant editor at the *Miami Herald*." Brandon's phone pinged, and he read the text. "Darn, Sara's on her way." He leaned in for a kiss. "You didn't get any of the walls measured."

She trailed a fingertip along his jawline. "Guess I'll have to come back sometime."

"Guess you will."

25

MORGAN CHECKED HERSELF once more in the full-length mirror. She'd splurged and bought a new outfit: a midnight blue scoop-neck top with three-quarter-length sleeves and a long, flowing skirt with a handkerchief hem and swirls of blue and silver throughout. Morgan loved how the skirt sparkled when she moved. Silver sandals and jewelry were the perfect complement. She enjoyed looking her best for Bran.

Morgan opened the door to his knock, and sucked in a breath. He looked like he'd stepped straight out of *GQ* in gray slacks, a navy blazer, and open-necked blue checked shirt.

"Happy birthday, babe," he said, sweeping her into his arms for a luscious kiss. "You look amazing."

"Thank you," she said breathlessly. "So do you." He smelled and felt wonderful. His aftershave or cologne had a heady, woodsy scent that Morgan was growing *very* fond of.

Bran pulled her close and kissed her again and again, as if he had all the time in the world. His lips trailed along her cheek to her neck. Morgan sighed. She felt incredibly beautiful and desired in a way that she had never experienced before.

He worked his way back to her mouth. "When does this *One Year* thing begin?" he said between kisses.

Morgan giggled. "It's *Four Seasons,* silly."

Brandon's eyes danced as he looked at her. "Which is—"

"One year," they said in unison.

Morgan laughed and picked up her purse. "Come on," she said. Brandon helped her into her jacket and they went out the door.

They arrived at the concert hall and found their seats about ten minutes before the concert began. Morgan saw some people that she knew, and was thrilled to introduce Brandon as her boyfriend. This day couldn't get any better. She opened her program and began to peruse it, and Brandon did the same.

"Now see, this is what I don't get," he said, pointing to something. "Tell me what that says."

Morgan wasn't sure what he was getting at. "Cello?"

"But what does c-e-l-l spell?"

She giggled. "Cell."

"Right," he said. "Like red and white blood cells. So why isn't c-e-l-l-o pronounced *sello?*"

Morgan laughed. "Bran, you're so cute."

The lights dimmed and the concert got underway. Brandon held her hand, and Morgan was so excited and proud to be here with him. This was the best birthday ever.

Well into the first half of the concert, the music reached a crescendo and Morgan was distracted by a movement out of the corner of her eye. A pregnant young woman sitting a few seats down in the row in front of them flinched. She and the man next to her laid their hands on her rounded belly and giggled and grinned at one another.

Morgan felt the breath leave her, and her eyes filled with tears. She would never feel a baby move inside her. She would never share that moment with the man she loved. Morgan reached for Bran's hand and was horrified to see that he was *asleep!* She nudged him and he startled awake. "Oh, sorry," he muttered. He rubbed his fingers over his mouth and sat up straighter, stifling a yawn.

Morgan turned away from him and wiped her eyes.

They went to the lobby during the break. "You need some caffeine," she said.

"I'm really sorry, Morgan. I had a long week." He did look tired, and Morgan tried not to be irritated with him. But really, falling asleep during a concert was terrible etiquette. And she was still out of sorts over the pregnant woman.

They returned to their seats for the second half, and when it had been underway only about five minutes, Brandon's pager started to buzz. He quickly turned it off and whispered to Morgan, "I'm sorry. Something must be up. Let me go make a phone call." He stood and crept along the row until he got to the aisle.

The couple next to Morgan looked at her disapprovingly. "He's a doctor," she whispered. Their sour expressions relaxed a bit.

Morgan had silenced her phone at the beginning of the concert, but she took it out in case Bran texted her. Sure enough, he did. *Babe, I'm so sorry. A patient developed complications and I've got to go in. I'll text you if I can wrap it up quickly and hopefully we can still do dinner.*

Morgan sighed. So much for the best birthday ever. *I understand, Bran,* she texted back. She tried to tamper her disappointment by reminding herself that this was life with a doctor.

When the concert concluded, she still hadn't heard from him, so Morgan took an Uber home. She changed into comfortable clothes, turned on the fireplace, and made a grilled cheese sandwich for dinner. She thought about what it would be like to have a child to celebrate her next birthday with, and decided then and there to call Joyce Sheldon the next day and get the process started.

She was feeling much better when Bran called just before nine o'clock. "Babe, I am so, so sorry," he said.

"Did you have to do surgery?"

"Yeah. We had to open a guy back up and do some repair work. He did too much, too soon. I just got out. Morgan, I promise I'll make it up to you. I had a gift for you and everything."

"Bran, it's okay. This wasn't your fault. But I'm not sure you were enjoying the concert that much, anyway." She tried to laugh to take the sting out of her comment.

"It was good, just not what I'm used to," he said. "Someday I'll take you to my kind of concert." He laughed.

"What? Some heavy metal thing?" she said teasingly.

"No, but you'll probably want to bring earplugs," he countered. They both laughed.

"I need to clean up and get home," Brandon said. "I mean it, Morgan, I'll make it up to you for tonight. Sweet dreams."

26

BRANDON STARTED THE car and turned out onto Michigan Avenue. He yawned. What a day. Not at all what he had hoped for. He really did feel badly about how Morgan's birthday turned out. Darla, of course, always understood when these things happened, but he wasn't sure Morgan would.

He needed some bro time, and speed-dialed Landon.

"Hey, bro," Landon answered.

"This a good time?"

"Yeah. I'm feeding my son a bottle. Let me put you on speaker. What are you doing?"

"Just finished a surgery, on my way home."

"On a Sunday night? Must not have been planned."

"You can say that again." Brandon gave his brother a quick summary of the surgery, and told him the name of the patient, who was a well-known athlete. He knew Landon would keep the information confidential.

Landon whistled. "Man, you sure travel in some high-class circles these days."

"I know. It's still hard to believe sometimes. Anyway, there's something I need to pick your brain about." He and Morgan had made a pact not to talk with Landon and Kelsea about their relationship, but he wasn't going to reveal anything. He just needed his brother's advice.

"I'm all ears," Landon said.

"Well, I've—hmm. Okay. I've started seeing someone."

"You don't say." His brother's voice didn't hold any censure.

"Yeah. I wasn't planning it. I didn't think I'd ever be interested in anyone again, but it just happened."

"What's her name?" Brandon heard the smile in his brother's voice.

Brandon smiled. "Nice try, bro. Not giving out any info right now."

Landon laughed. "Okay."

"It's only a couple of weeks in. Anyway, the thing is, we're not at all alike. I mean—like not at all. She doesn't follow sports *at all*." Brandon knew his brother would understand the significance of this more than anyone else. "But we find things to talk about. I could talk with her forever. And she's beautiful, inside and out."

"And she's a great kisser," Landon added.

"And she's a great kisser," Brandon repeated. He sighed. "Man, is she ever." He thought about how gorgeous Morgan looked this afternoon and the potent kisses they'd shared. He wished they could have skipped the boring concert.

"Sounds like you're hooked."

"Yeah, I think I am. But it's so weird. I try not to compare her to Dar, but it's hard. We loved all the same things. I just haven't found any common ground yet with—"

Landon jumped right in. "With who? Say that again? I think you were breaking up there for a moment," he teased.

"Nice try!" The two brothers chuckled. "Oh, I'm fine," Brandon said. "I just, I don't know, I just wanted to share it with you."

"I'm glad you did," Landon said. "Give it some time, and it'll either work out, or it won't."

"Gee, bro, that's brilliant. Let me write that down," Brandon said drily.

The two brothers laughed. "I'm really glad you've decided to rejoin life," Landon said.

"You don't think it's too soon?"

"No, I don't. Do you really see yourself raising April and Shelbie by yourself, and then being all alone in twenty years when they leave home?"

"I haven't really thought that far," Brandon admitted. "Until very recently, I've been focused on getting through one day at a time." He sighed. "But I know I don't want to spend the rest of my life alone. It's just been hard to admit that. You know, it feels a little like I'm being unfaithful to Darla's memory." He swallowed around the lump in his throat.

"What would Dar tell you to do?" Landon asked.

Brandon snorted softly. "She'd kick my butt and tell me to grab life by the horns and make it count."

"Exactly. It's all part of the healing process," Landon said quietly. "Just take it one step at a time. And I'll be praying for you."

They went on to talk about the twins and other things, and Landon told him that he and his family were definitely going to Wisconsin for Thanksgiving.

"Great, the girls and Peanut and I will be there, too."

"You won't believe how much the babies have grown," Landon said.

"I'll bet! Well, thanks for being there for me. I'll see you in a few weeks."

"Hey, bro, did you and Morgan ever get together?"

Brandon almost drove off the road. "What?"

"You know, did Morgan ever get back to look at your house for artwork and all that stuff?"

His heartrate returned to normal. "Oh—yeah. She's coming to measure walls. Sometime. I'm not sure when." Brandon hoped he had his story straight.

"Oh, that's good," Landon said. "Well, talk to you soon. Love ya, man"

"Love ya, man." Brandon disconnected. *Whew. That was close.*

27

MORGAN HELD OUT until Tuesday night, and then called her sister.

"Can you talk for a little while?" she asked.

"Morgy, are you okay?" Kelsea was the protective, older sister and was always afraid that something was drastically wrong.

"I'm fine, I just need some sister time."

"Okay. Let me do a couple of things and get Landon on baby watch and I'll call you right back."

"Don't tell him anything," Morgan said.

"What do you mean? I just need to make sure he'll look after the twins. I'll call you right back." Kelsea disconnected without another word.

Morgan let out a sigh. Maybe this wasn't such a good idea. Then she scolded herself. *Keep it vague. She won't figure anything out unless you reveal too much.* She sat down at her kitchen table and drummed her fingers until the phone rang.

"Hi," she said.

"Morgy, are you sure you're okay? What's going on?"

"Kels, I'm *fine,*" Morgan said with emphasis. "I'm just—well, I wanted to tell you that I—I'm sort of dating someone."

She heard her sister gasp. "That's wonderful! What's his name?"

Morgan rolled her eyes. "Oh no. This is still very new and I'm not going to jinx it."

"Are you back with Patrick?"

"What? No!" Now that Brandon was in her life, Morgan couldn't figure out what she had ever seen in Patrick.

"Where did you meet him? What does he do?" Kelsea bubbled in her typical way.

Not on your life, sister. "It doesn't matter, Kels," Morgan said firmly. She was bound and determined not to leave any bread crumbs for her sister to follow.

"What does he look like? Morgy! Is he *TDH*?"

Morgan laughed joyously. She could go down this road. "Oh, Kels, he's *so* TDH!" Kelsea laughed with her. "And he's just—he's *completely* different from Patrick. He makes me feel things that I've never felt before." Her voice had gotten quieter.

"Is he a good kisser?"

"Mmm, the best. I've—I've *never* been kissed like this."

"Sounds like you're in love, Morgy."

"What?" Morgan's heart began to trip. "No, I'm not—it's, I've only known him for a very short time."

Kelsea gave a dry laugh. "True love doesn't know what a clock or a calendar is, Morgy. Take it from the expert."

Morgan had to give her sister that one. Landon and Kelsea had met under very unusual circumstances and were legally married just eight days later, but they didn't know it. Then they went their separate ways and were reunited three weeks later, got engaged, and stayed married. It was one of the most unusual love stories ever.

"I know. But this is so different, Kelsea. Every minute of my life is filled with him. When I'm with him, it's incredible, and when I'm not with him, I can hardly breathe. We never run out of things to talk about, but we're so different."

"You and Patrick were too much alike, Morgan."

"I know that now. But this guy—Kels, he knows *nothing* about the arts. He went with me to a symphonic wind concert for my birthday and fell asleep before the intermission!"

Kelsea laughed. "I'd fall asleep at one of those concerts, too. What's he into? Wait—let me guess. Sports?"

Revealing that won't be a bread crumb. Half the men in Chicago are TDH and into sports. "Yes, big time. But it's not just that. He's really outgoing, and loves noise and crowds, and you know me, how much I like my calm, quiet life."

"Maybe you need to come out of your shell a little," Kelsea said softly.

"Maybe I do." Morgan sighed. "And I don't know whether or when I should tell him about my infertility."

"I know, it's hard. Morgan, I know that's what ended things with Patrick, but his reaction was proof that he wasn't worth it. He wasn't the guy for you. And you'll know when it's the right time to tell *this* guy, and if he's the right one, it won't matter to him. He'll love you no matter what."

Morgan felt close to tears. "You're probably right. Anyway, I just had to tell someone."

"I'm glad it was me, Morgy," Kelsea said warmly.

"Well, who else would I tell?" Morgan said with a laugh. "You can't tell Landon," she begged.

"Why not?"

Morgan couldn't think of an answer that she could tell her sister. "Well, it's still so new. Just don't say anything until I know if this is going to take."

"Not trying to be pushy," Kelsea ventured, "but what does this do to your plan to foster or adopt?"

Morgan sighed. "I'm not sure. That's another thing I'm confused about. I've been playing phone tag with a woman who's the one to help me get all the paperwork going. So that's stalled, and I guess I just need to pray about it."

"I'll keep praying, too," Kelsea assured her.

Morgan changed the subject. "What are you guys doing for Thanksgiving?" Of course, she already had a good idea.

"We're going to Landon's parents in Wisconsin. I think Brandon and his girls and Sara are coming, too."

"Well, if Mom doesn't go to Uncle Steve's, I should go home to be with her." The prospect of spending the holiday weekend in Kankakee filled Morgan with dread.

"You and Mom should come to Wisconsin!" Kelsea exclaimed as if she had just discovered the secret to the fountain of youth. "Unless you can't stand the thought of being around *Dr. Moron,*" she said with a chuckle.

Morgan nearly burst into hysterical laughter. She would have to come clean with Bran about that. "I suppose I can put up with him in order to see my niece and nephew." She hoped she sounded convincing. "Are you sure your in-laws won't mind?"

"I'm sure they'd love to have you. They have a huge house with room for everyone. I'll set it up."

Morgan smiled. *Was it really going to be that easy?* "Um, I guess," she said, trying to act like it wasn't the best idea ever.

"I want to see you, Morgy," Kelsea said. "You won't believe how big the babies have gotten."

That was something Morgan could get excited for. "Okay, then. You'll talk to Mom?"

"I'll talk to Mom. I'll see you in a few weeks!"

"Thanks for the sister talk, Sissy. Love you."

"Always. Love you back. Oh, Morgan! Did you ever get together with Brandon?"

Morgan almost dropped the phone. "Huh? What?" she stammered.

"You know. Did you ever get back over to his house to look at some ideas for artwork?"

Morgan smiled to herself. Oh, she'd gotten back to Brandon's house, but they always found something else to do rather than measure walls and talk about decorating. "Ah—yeah. I went back once and did some measuring. Gotta go, Kels. See you soon!"

28

BRANDON HAD BEEN trying to think of a way to make it up to Morgan for blowing it on her birthday, and the perfect opportunity may have just been handed to him.

Steve Lambetti was standing in the door of his office and had just invited him to fly with the Blackhawks to a game in Toronto on Sunday.

"Can I bring a date?" he asked.

"Sure," Lambetti replied.

"It's a turnaround trip, right?" Brandon was getting an idea of how these things worked.

"Yeah, we'll get home late, but we'll get to sleep in our own beds. We'll fly out of Midway Sunday morning. I'll text you the gate number and departure time. Don't forget your passport."

"Thanks, Steve."

He immediately texted Morgan. *Do you have a passport, babe?* If she didn't, that would nix his whole plan. She didn't reply right away, and he looked at his watch. It was

Thursday, which meant she was in a session. Two hours later, his phone rang when he was on the way home.

"Okay, you've got my attention," she said, with no preamble.

He laughed. "So, do you have a passport? And are you okay with flying?"

"Yes to both," she replied. He could tell she was about to explode with curiosity.

"Well, then, are you free on Sunday?"

"Bran! What in the world do you have planned? I can't go jetting off halfway across the world on Sunday. I have classes to teach on Monday."

"Who said anything about going halfway across the world?" he said coyly.

"Well, now you *really* have me flummoxed," she said.

"Flummoxed? Who uses that word?" he teased.

"Okay, then. Bewildered. Perplexed. So curious, I'm about to pass out!"

Brandon laughed again. "You're adorable, babe. This is to make up for messing up your birthday. I promise I'll have you home by midnight."

Her sigh rippled into his ear. "If you were here, I'll bet I could kiss you into telling me where we're going."

His heart skipped a beat. "I'm sure you could. So, what do you say?"

"Bran, this is crazy. I don't do crazy things. Are you sure I'll be back by Monday? I have a really full day."

Brandon thought about the trips he'd taken over the past two months on the various private jets and chartered planes. No airport security, no lines, no delayed or canceled flights. "I promise, you'll be back by Monday."

"What should I wear?"

"Well, it's November, so wear whatever you would wear in Chicago in November."

"So, no tropics," Morgan said. "We must be heading north."

"I didn't say that," Brandon replied. "You're a sneaky one, Dr. Anderson."

Her laugh sounded like wind chimes. "I'll see you Sunday."

"No, you'll see me tomorrow night. You're coming for dinner and to measure the walls or something, remember?"

"Oh, yes. I thought—did I measure the walls already?"

"You sound flummoxed, babe."

She giggled again. "Oh, no, I didn't. So yes, I'll come to dinner tomorrow night and measure some walls."

"I just pulled in the garage. See you tomorrow night."

"Bye, Bran."

29

MORGAN COULDN'T BELIEVE it. They were flying to Canada on a chartered plane with the Chicago Blackhawks! That *was* crazy, and as she'd told Bran on the phone the other night, she didn't do crazy.

But hadn't her sister said just the other night on the phone that Morgan needed to come out of her shell?

Morgan loved sitting with Bran, holding his hand, and when he introduced her to various coaches and players as his girlfriend. She could tell he was popular with everyone. They gave him fist bumps and high fives and called him "Doc."

The game was the noisiest event Morgan had ever experienced, even louder than the basketball game. "Canadians really love their hockey," Bran shouted into her ear at one point. It was almost impossible to carry on a conversation. But the Blackhawks won, so the home fans weren't as noisy at the end.

After the game, Bran said they may as well sit and relax.

They weren't going anywhere until the players had showered and dressed. There were two players' wives along for the trip, and Morgan chatted with them for a little while. They told her that more wives and children traveled with the team when it was an overnight trip, but since this was just a quick day trip, most had stayed home.

When they finally left the arena and trooped out to the chartered bus, they were surprised to see that it was snowing, and had been for some time. Morgan wondered nervously if the weather might delay their flight. But when they got to the airport they were ushered right onto the plane, and her fears abated.

They got settled in their seats and buckled in. Brandon squeezed Morgan's hand. "Thank you for coming with me. I hope this made up for your birthday."

"It was wonderful, Bran, thank you," Morgan said.

She looked out the window where the snow swirled around them. "I wonder why we aren't going yet?"

"Hmm, I don't know," Brandon replied. "Maybe they're going to deice us."

"I hope we don't get home too late. My day tomorrow is insane, packed from beginning to end." Morgan yawned and laid her head on his shoulder.

The most important reason for Morgan to be back in Chicago tomorrow was for an early morning meeting with Joyce Sheldon to begin the process of becoming a foster parent. They had finally connected and just got their calendars to sync. Morgan was fortunate that Joyce had worked her in, but now she wasn't even sure if this was the right time to move forward, given her new relationship with Bran, and she still hadn't said anything to him about it, and didn't know if she should. She was torn because being with him and the girls made her want a family of her own even more, but it didn't feel like the right time to bring it up with him. She didn't want him to think that she was dating him in order to get a ready-made family.

The pilot's voice came on over the intercom. "Good evening, folks. An update from the cockpit. This storm moved in more quickly than they anticipated, but they think we can get out. We're next for deicing and then we should be cleared for takeoff. We'll keep you updated."

"See? We'll be fine," Brandon said, and squeezed Morgan's hand. After a few minutes, he looked over her shoulder out the window and they watched the deicing process together. Then the plane backed out of the gate and rolled across the tarmac and stopped.

And sat. And sat some more. Morgan began to grow restless.

The pilot came on again. "Sorry, folks. We need to go back to be deiced again, and then they're going to try to get us out."

"I don't like this, Bran," Morgan whispered.

He pulled her close. "We'll be fine, babe," he murmured. They sat and cuddled while the process was repeated, and then the plane rolled out again.

Twenty minutes later, Morgan felt the plane turn around and head back toward the terminal. She could tell by looking out the window that it was almost whiteout conditions.

"Well, folks, you can probably tell that we're headed back to the gate," the pilot said. They've closed the airport, so we'll deplane and try again in the morning." A wave of grunts rolled through the cabin.

Morgan's eyes widened. "Bran! We're not going home? I have to be home tonight!"

Brandon tried to quiet her. "Babe, I'm so sorry."

"I can't believe I did this. I never should have come."

"Morgan, I'm sorry, I didn't think about a weather delay."

"This is terrible!" She pulled away from him and wrung her hands. "I just need a moment to think."

Brandon didn't reply. Most of the players had gone to sleep, and now woke up and shuffled off the plane. When they got back in the terminal, a man that Bran said was the front office rep gathered everyone around. He'd just gotten off his phone. "Sorry for the inconvenience, everyone. I've just been talking with the airport authority folks, and they're following this system closely and think they'll be able to get planes back in the air by six a.m., so we want to keep everyone here and board by five or five-thirty. This will be our gate. Since we don't go through TSA, you need to stay in this wing of the terminal. There's not much open, but they've opened up a coffee shop down that way on the left, and we'll run a tab." He pointed back over everyone's heads.

There were grumbles all around and one of the players called out, "Can they open a bar and you run a tab there, Bill?"

Everyone laughed. "Sorry, no," Bill said. "You know the rules, guys."

The group began to disperse and Brandon turned to Morgan. "I'm so sorry, Morgan." He took her hand. "It's a two-hour flight, so we'll come close to making it home by morning."

"But I'll be all stinky and rumpled in these clothes," she

complained. "By the time I get home, take a shower, and get to my—where I need to be, it will be too late."

"Morgan, I'm sorry. What can I do—"

She waved him off. "I need to get on the phone," she said, and walked away from him. She knew there was no way he could have foreseen this, and she was angrier at herself for taking off on a lark than she was at him.

It took her about fifteen minutes to make all the arrangements. She'd left a voicemail for Joyce, canceling their meeting and apologizing profusely. Morgan hated canceling appointments. She was always afraid that it left an impression that she wasn't organized and reliable. She feared that Joyce would think she wasn't responsible enough to care for a child.

"I have my morning covered," she said to Brandon. "It wasn't easy. And those international minutes are going to make my phone bill skyrocket." He held out his arms to her, and she came to him. "No more crazy outings with you," she scolded.

He rubbed noses with her. "I'll pay your phone bill. Can I kiss my way back into your good graces?" he murmured, running his lips up under her ear and around to her neck.

Morgan squirmed away from him and stilled his hands. "We're in public, Bran," she said with a twinkle in her eye.

He wrapped his arm around her and began to walk. "Then let me buy you a cup of coffee."

30

MORGAN OPENED HER eyes and stretched. The first thought that popped into her mind was *it's Friday*. The second one caused a delicious quiver to start in her stomach and spread outward. *I'll see him tonight.*

The Canada debacle didn't turn out as badly as Morgan had first anticipated. They got off just before six o'clock and the pilots pushed them along to make good time. Bran ordered an Uber for her and it was waiting when they landed in Chicago. Since they didn't have to deal with customs or baggage claim, that saved some time. Morgan got home, showered, changed, and was on campus by nine o'clock.

The best part about the whole trip was sitting up all night with Bran in the airport, first in the little coffee shop, and then in a quiet corner of the terminal with the snowstorm raging all around them. She apologized for being so upset, and they held hands and talked about everything under the sun. Morgan felt like they were in their own little romantic cocoon. Everyone around them was asleep or not paying them the least bit of attention, and they got some really nice kissing breaks in.

Then, on the plane, Morgan slept in his arms, and he treated her to a spectacular wake-up kiss as the sun came up outside the window.

He filled her thoughts constantly, and when they weren't together, when their schedules allowed, they were either on the phone or texting back and forth. The last week and a half had flown by, mostly due to Morgan being tied up with an art show. But Brandon had also been away on a trip and she had only seen him once this week, for lunch on Wednesday. They were both busy yesterday and couldn't get their schedules to mesh. He'd invited her to the house for dinner again tonight—this time under the guise of coming to look at the rooms and walls and begin figuring what kinds of art and other decorative items would go best, now that she had measured them. She couldn't wait to see him—and the girls and Sara—tonight.

But then, the thought that was never far from her mind settled around her like a dark cloud and dampened her enthusiasm. Was it time to tell him about her infertility issues? Morgan nibbled on her thumbnail. It was a horrible conundrum. They'd only been together for a little over a month, but it felt like forever. There was never a place in the conversation to insert, "oh, by the way, I can't have children," and bringing up something so personal and with such obvious implications for a long-term commitment was a huge risk.

One she hadn't taken with Patrick, and it cost her dearly.

She'd met Patrick Carrington in the fall four years ago in the library at UIC—University of Illinois, Chicago—when she'd gone to pick up some books for a research project. She was staring at a wonderful Monet, and he'd stopped and they began to chat about it. That led to coffee. Over the next month they had lunch, dinner, or coffee at least once a week, went to a symphonic concert, and an art show. And lots of walks. Patrick loved to walk along the shoreline of Lake Michigan.

He was an Assistant Professor of English Literature at UIC. He was tall—though not as tall as Brandon—and slim with sandy blond hair and bright blue eyes. He was quiet and thoughtful, and by the end of their first month together, he'd held her hand several times, but hadn't kissed Morgan even once.

When the city got its first snow on a Sunday afternoon, he called and invited her on a walk. It was a soft, gentle snowfall with big, fat flakes and an uncharacteristic absence of Chicago's notorious wind. And then, Patrick had kissed her for the first time, and Morgan thought she might really be falling for him.

They continued walking, and soon passed a family—a mom, dad, and two small children, a boy and a girl, all holding hands. The children were catching snowflakes on their tongues and squealing, and the parents were laughing with them. Patrick turned to Morgan and said, "They look so happy, don't they? Maybe that will be us one day."

Morgan stopped and began to weep, and Patrick frowned at her. "Morgan, what's wrong?"

In halting sentences, she explained to him about her medical condition and the likelihood that she would never bear children. Morgan hoped that he would take her in his arms and assure her that it was okay, and that they would work through it together. She was in no way prepared for what he said next.

"Oh, dear. I—I certainly didn't expect that." He glared at her. "Didn't you think that was something important enough to share with me right up front? I feel like you've been dishonest with me, Morgan. Are there other things you're holding back?"

Suffice to say, the conversation went downhill from there. When Patrick began talking about how important it was to his parents that he carry on the Carrington bloodline, Morgan knew that their budding relationship had withered and died.

That was the last day she saw or heard from him, and she hadn't sought out or encouraged anyone since.

Morgan sighed. There was a definite spark with Brandon that had never been present with Patrick, who had been too much like Morgan—quiet and deliberate. His kiss was nice. Brandon's kisses set her on fire. From the moment his lips touched hers, she wanted more.

What was she going to do? Tell him now, or later? Morgan knew deep down that there was too much to lose if she made the wrong choice.

She was still conflicted about whether to tell Bran about her desire to bring a child into her life. But the more Morgan worked with the arts program in Chicago, the more she fell in love with the children. She'd felt terrible about having to cancel her appointment with Joyce, and hadn't heard back from her yet about rescheduling. Was this God's way of closing the door? Morgan wasn't sure if she should try to make contact again, or wait for Joyce to make the next move. She hoped the woman wasn't mad and had decided to give up on Morgan.

She got up and checked her phone, then sat up and

reached for her devotional book. For years, Morgan had started her day with a dose of God's Word. It was the perfect way to fill up for the day ahead. She asked Him for wisdom about how to handle both of her dilemmas.

When Morgan came out of the shower, she found a missed call and a text from Brandon, and as she read it, her heart sank. *Gotta fly to LA to do a surgery, dinner will have to wait until later in the weekend. I'm so sorry. I'll call you when I know more. I can't wait to see you. Saving up all of my kisses* ☺

Morgan sighed and ran her fingers over the word *kisses.* This man was almost too good to be true. But maybe this was her answer. It would buy her some time to make a decision about what to tell him, and when.

She got through her busy day and grabbed her phone every time it made a noise. It was after four o'clock and she had just arrived home when he finally called. "Babe, I'm so sorry I had to cancel our plans, and that it took me so long to call. Surgery took longer than expected, and now I've been asked to consult on another case up in San Francisco. I probably won't get home until sometime on Sunday."

Morgan could already see the long, lonely weekend stretching out in front of her. "It's okay, Bran," she said. "I'll let you make it up to me." It still surprised her how the bold, flirtatious words came to her so easily these days.

"I absolutely will," he whispered. "And in less than a week, we'll have five whole days together for Thanksgiving. I can't wait." No one knew that Morgan was driving up with them. They were going to concoct a story about her car having issues at the last minute so that she would have to catch a ride to Wisconsin with Brandon, Sara, and the girls.

And no one had any inkling about the bombshell that Brandon and Morgan were going to drop on everyone once they got there.

Morgan's stomach did flips. "I can't wait to see the look on Kelsea's face when we tell everyone about us."

Brandon laughed. "And Landon's."

"And Sara's," they said in unison, and then they laughed together.

"I hope April and Shelbie will approve," Morgan said softly.

"Morgan, they'll be so excited, you know they will," Brandon said. "Oh, here comes a nurse looking for me. I have to go."

"She'd better not be beautiful," Morgan warned him.

"She's sixty with buck teeth and warts all over her face," Brandon said teasingly. Morgan laughed. "I'll text or call you when I can, babe. Have a good weekend."

"You, too. See you soon."

Morgan set her phone down and smiled to herself. What to do with all this time now? Maybe she would just go to Luke and Miranda's cabin for the weekend and paint. She looked at the clock. Even if she hurried to pack, she'd hit the heavy weekend outbound traffic. She went into her bedroom and stood in front of her dresser. "I'll go in the morning," she said to her reflection. It was perfect. She'd have two full days there to paint, recharge her batteries, and sort out her feelings about Brandon and their possible future.

Morgan went to bed early and hit the road early the next morning. She unpacked her things and was painting by nine o'clock. She turned her phone off (the service was spotty anyway) and immersed herself in the work—which wasn't really work to her, but soothing therapy. She'd texted Miranda and they were out of town at her in-laws' for the weekend, so Morgan was completely alone, which was fine with her. Solitude was different from loneliness, and Morgan loved her solitude.

When she took a break for lunch, she turned her phone back on and saw that there was a missed call from Brandon. She walked around the perimeter of the cabin, hoping to get service, but no luck. For some reason it was worse than usual. She began to text him but figured with no service, why bother?

Morgan packed a few supplies and decided to take a walk. It was a gorgeous late fall day and she was inspired by the muted colors and autumn scents. The temperature was perfect and the breeze was gentle. Morgan felt herself unwinding.

She hiked through the woods and found a beautiful spot next to a little creek, and set up her things. Before dusk settled, she packed everything up and headed back to the cabin and had a simple supper of some crackers, cheese, and grapes. She checked her phone again but there was no service.

After a while, Morgan built a fire, then went outside and sat on the porch to watch the sun set, and then the stars came out. Millions—no, billions—of stars glittered down on her. Morgan sighed deeply. This was what she loved about the country. It fed her soul. She loved the rich cultural aspects of living in the city, but sometimes, it sucked the life out of her. She sat there, deep in thought, and wondered if she could find a happy medium. The problem was, her work was in the city, and she didn't know if she wanted to take on the tiresome commute.

She sat there for another hour, and her thoughts wandered to Brandon. What if things progressed between them to a permanent relationship? Morgan couldn't imagine living in his million-dollar home. Even with some of the ideas she had about how to decorate it, the new, contemporary style didn't fit her at all. The wealthy suburb in which it sat wasn't at all Morgan's cup of tea, either. Brandon was beginning to express doubts about it, too, but he said he was a "city boy" and if he decided to make a move, it would be that way.

"This is something else I need to pray about, right, Lord?" Morgan said to the heavens. She decided to go inside, fix a cup of cocoa, and paint some more. She did some of her best work late into the night.

She saw her phone on the counter and checked it once again. Now she had service, and Morgan was stunned to see *fifteen* missed calls from Brandon, seven voice messages, and twelve texts! What in the world? Had something happened to him, or the girls? Morgan's heart went into overdrive.

31

BRANDON WAS BESIDE himself. *Where was Morgan? Why wasn't she picking up?* He didn't have a key to her condo, and he'd been banging on the door for twenty minutes. He walked back out to his SUV and texted her again. *Babe, where are you? Call me, Morgan. Please, please call me.*

Brandon was beginning to feel like he was getting right with God again, but this was testing his faith. His heart felt like it was about to bang out of his chest. *If anything happens to her, I don't know how I could*—his phone rang and he grabbed it.

"Oh, Morgan! Thank God. Where are you?" he shouted.

"I'm at a friend's farm. Bran, I'm so sorry, the service out here is terrible. Are you okay? Are the girls okay?"

"Yes, yes. I just—" Brandon gulped in air. "I'm sitting outside your condo. I ended up not having to go to San Francisco, so I flew back to surprise you. But I—I just couldn't imagine why you weren't here. And then when you didn't pick up, I was afraid—" His throat closed.

"Oh, Bran. I'm so sorry."

"Morgan, I'm coming to you. Text me the address." The words spilled out in a rush.

"Bran, it'll take you almost ninety minutes. Why don't I meet you—"

"No!" he shouted. "Morgan, don't go—don't go *anywhere*. Don't move—babe, *please*, stay right there. I'll come to you."

She sounded worried. "Bran, are you sure you're okay to drive?"

"I'm fine. I'm already on my way. Text me the address, quick, in case you lose service again."

"Okay, I'm hanging up now and I'll text you." She followed through on that promise, and then called him back. "Did you get my text?"

"Yes," he said, and they talked for a while longer. He felt better, and Morgan began asking him questions about the surgery. He figured she was trying to keep him focused and calm. But after about twenty minutes, the call dropped, and he couldn't get through to her again.

32

ONCE SHE LOST service, Morgan spent the next hour putting her painting supplies away and trying in vain to get service on her phone, and finally took a blanket out on the porch and wrapped up in it to wait for Brandon. The stars kept her company and she talked to God, too.

When she saw headlights coming up the gravel drive, she ran to the SUV. Brandon cut the engine, tumbled out, and swept her into his arms.

"Morgan, oh babe," he murmured. She heard him take a deep breath, and choke back a sob. He held her so tightly, she could hardly breathe. Then he was kissing her desperately, and she could feel tears on his cheeks. He whispered her name over and over and stood there, just holding her and rocking back and forth. "I can't do this, I can't do this," he sobbed.

"Can't do what, Bran?" She stepped back and cupped his wet cheeks in her hands. His handsome face was ravaged with pain.

"I can't—I—if anything ever happened to you—" He all

but fell on her, sobbing. "I couldn't go through that again. I couldn't."

Morgan's heart broke for him. "Let's go sit on the porch swing," she said quietly, and led him there and pulled the blanket around them. He wrapped her in his arms and they sat there for a long time, not saying anything, just rocking. Then she felt his lips on her hair.

Brandon drew back and stared at her. Starlight shone down on them like diamond dust, and filtered light from inside the cabin spilled across his features. As she looked into his eyes, Morgan's heart melted, and at that moment she knew what he was going to say, and exactly how she was going to respond.

He spoke so softly, Morgan could hardly hear him. "I was going to say that I can't love you, Morgan. But it's too late. I'm already so in love with you." He leaned in and touched his lips to hers. "So in love with you," he whispered.

"Oh, Bran," she said softly, cradling his face in her hands. "I love you with all my heart." And their next kiss was like nothing Morgan had ever known, and tears of joy bubbled up and ran down her cheeks. Brandon's kisses were so sweet and beautiful, and then Morgan's joy turned to fear, and she began to sob.

"Sweetheart, Morgan, what's wrong?" Brandon looked at her, his eyes dark with worry.

"I—oh, Bran, I have to tell you something," she sobbed, covering her face with her hands. *I waited too long.* "Something I should have told you right away, but it's—I—" Morgan didn't know how she was going to tell him.

He swallowed, and she could see the panic in his eyes. "Are you married? Are you sick? Are—"

Morgan gasped. She grabbed his hands and squeezed. "No, no! Oh, Bran, no. I'm so sorry—I'm not handling this right—"

He tenderly touched her face. "Please, just tell me. Whatever it is, we'll get through it together, Morgan. I love you so much. Whatever's wrong, it doesn't matter."

Morgan took a deep, shaky breath, and then her story came out, haltingly at first, and then in a river of tears and rushing words.

"Shh, shh," Brandon whispered. "It's okay, babe. It doesn't matter. I mean it, I mean it." He held her tighter. "It wasn't something you needed to tell me until it felt like the right time to *you*."

"I—it's just not something you bring up on a first date, or a second date. But then—Bran, now you're *stuck* with this—and your girls want a little brother. I won't hold you—"

He cut her words off with a deep, passionate kiss. "Oh, Bran," she whispered.

He gazed at her. "Morgan, if things keep going, and we get to that place, we'll already have a family."

"I know, but—"

He shook his head. "No buts. How do you feel about the girls?"

Morgan spoke without even thinking "Oh, Bran. I love them like they were my own—" She stopped and felt her jaw drop.

He tilted his head at her. "See? And there are all kinds of ways to grow a family." He kissed her and touched his forehead to hers. "God works these things out."

She nodded. *Should I tell him about my hope to foster or*

adopt? No, this wasn't the time. She'd already hit him with enough big news. The breeze kicked up and she shivered. "Would you like to go inside?"

He nodded, and followed her in. Morgan realized that she'd never fixed her cocoa, and asked Bran if he'd like that, or coffee. She felt badly that she didn't have his favorite kind at the cabin, but she hadn't expected him to be there.

"Cocoa sounds good," he said.

She fixed their mugs and joined him on the couch in front of the fire. When they'd finished, Bran pulled her close, and she curled up with her head on his chest, listening to the steady sound of his heartbeat. Morgan thought she could stay here just like this for the next fifty years.

After a while she looked up at him. "Tell me about Darla," she whispered.

"You sure?"

Morgan nodded.

He was silent for a few moments. "Well, I met her in Chemistry our junior year of high school. We were assigned as lab partners. She was a little thing—only about five foot one, and she always struggled with her weight a bit." He shrugged. "I told her it didn't matter." He fingered Morgan's hair. "Her hair was about the same color as yours, and she wore it long most of the time, pulled back in a ponytail. She was pretty low maintenance." He smiled. "Your hair is thick. Hers wasn't."

"Did she always want to be a doctor?" Morgan asked.

Brandon nodded. "Yep. A lot of med students don't choose their specialties until they're done with rotations, but she always knew she wanted to be a neurosurgeon." He shook his head. "She was one of the best. We went to college and then med school together. She was—I tell you, what she lacked in size, she made up for in determination." He smiled. "She was from Dallas. Her family moved north when she was thirteen, and she had a personality as big and bold as Texas. I would go to watch her surgeries whenever I could. She ran her OR like a drill sergeant, but everyone loved and respected her. She was really something. So outgoing and full of life. Not afraid of anything."

Morgan smiled. "Sounds like Shelbie."

Brandon nodded. "Yes, Shelbie is very much like her mother." He pressed his forehead against Morgan's and took her hand. "She'll never know her," he whispered. "She'll never remember."

Morgan put her arms around him. "I'm sorry," she murmured. They sat like that for a while and then Brandon cleared his throat.

"I want to tell you about that night," he said softly.

"Only if you're sure," Morgan said. She felt him nod.

Brandon took a deep breath. "We had a shortage of orthopedic surgeons at the hospital, and I had been working long hours for about three months. Then they hired another guy, and it started to ease up a little bit. I finally got a night off, and we were at home with the girls." He swallowed. "Dar needed a few things from the store and I offered to go, but she said since I'd missed so many nights at home, why didn't I do the girls' baths and story time and put them to bed." His eyes grew moist. "I—ah, she blew me a kiss, said 'love y'all,' like she always did, and I said the same thing back, and she went out the door and—and that was it."

Morgan squeezed his hands.

"We each had an SUV," he said, "but we still had this

little Triumph convertible that had been our first car in college. After April came along, we couldn't all fit in it, so it mostly sat in the garage, but we had such great memories and couldn't bear to part with it."

Brandon stared off into the distance. "It was a beautiful early June evening, and Dar decided to take it. She loved to fly along in it with the top down." He shrugged and shook his head sadly. "There was a wide, downhill curve a couple of miles from our house. She took it too fast and lost control. She was wearing a seat belt but the car flipped and she—she died instantly." He closed his eyes.

"It happened on her way there, just a few minutes after she'd left, I wasn't even expecting her back yet when the doorbell rang." He swallowed. "When I saw the two policemen standing on my front porch, I knew." Tears ran down his cheeks. "My first call was to Landon. He caught the last flight out of St. Louis that night. Stayed with me for over a week. I couldn't have gotten through it without him."

Morgan got up and brought him a handful of tissues.

He blotted at his eyes. "It's taken me a long time to come to grips with the fact that it was just one of those things, that it wasn't my fault."

She took his hand. "Of course it wasn't your fault, Bran."

"I know. But when something like this happens, we want someone or something to blame. They checked out the car thoroughly to see if it was a mechanical issue. I had hung my hopes on that, but there wasn't a thing wrong with it."

Brandon drew Morgan into his arms, and they talked long into the night, about faith and family and relationships and all sorts of things. She'd never felt so close to another human being in all her life.

The next thing Morgan knew, it was morning, and Bran was kissing her awake.

33

BRANDON BURIED HIS face in her neck. She was so warm and soft, and her hair was like silk and smelled like something heady and floral, not her normal shampoo. This was the absolute best way to start the day. His mouth moved across her cheek to her soft, full lips, and he sighed and pulled her closer.

"Oh, Bran," she whispered.

Brandon froze. His heart leapt into his throat. *Morgan.* They'd fallen asleep on the couch. He sat up and scooted away from her.

"Bran, what's wrong?"

"Nothing, I—I'll be right back." He jumped up and made a beeline for the bathroom.

Brandon closed the door behind him and leaned against the sink. His heart still pounded. He put the toilet seat cover down and sat with his head in his hands. *Dear God.* How could this have happened? It didn't take a genius to figure out that after all the emotions of last night, that he'd—that he must have been dreaming of Darla. But how could he—*I love Morgan,* he told himself. *I do. I know I do.*

Does she know? How will I ever fix this? If she doesn't know, should I tell her? I don't want to keep secrets from her. The thoughts pinged around his head like it was a pinball machine.

Finally, he stood and splashed water on his face and rinsed out his mouth. Brandon took a deep breath. *Help me, God,* he prayed as he reached for the door handle.

The aroma of freshly brewed coffee assaulted him. Morgan was standing at the sink with a mug, staring out the window. She turned and looked at him, and there wasn't a doubt in Brandon's mind.

She knew.

Brandon took careful, quiet steps toward the kitchen. He saw another mug sitting on the counter, but coffee was the last thing on his mind right now. He continued walking toward Morgan until he was just a few feet away from her. He felt like he was approaching a skittish animal who might bolt at any second.

She set her mug down on the counter and folded her hands in front of her.

"I'm so sorry, Morgan," he whispered. He waited for her to scream at him, or tell him to leave. But what she did next completely shocked him.

She held out her hand, and he took it. "It's—it's okay, Bran," she whispered. A tear escaped and rolled down her cheek.

"Oh, babe," he whispered, and broke into tears himself. She was so beautiful, so forgiving, and Brandon felt like the most horrible man on earth for causing her this pain.

They moved at the same time and were in each other's arms. They stood there for a long time, just holding one another. Then he took her by the hand and led her back to the couch and pulled her close.

"I meant what I said last night, Morgan. I love you. I don't know how—"

She put a finger to his lips. "She was your wife for almost fifteen years," Morgan said. "She's been in your life for half of it. She's the mother of your children." Brandon saw her swallow. "She will always be a part of you." She gave him a sad little smile. "I just have to learn to accept it. And I will." She let out a slow stream of air. "I'll be okay."

Brandon tried to think how he would feel if the tables were turned, and his gratitude for Morgan's love and understanding took a herculean leap. He brushed a lock of hair off her face. "Telling you everything last night was emotional for me," he said. "It was really the first time that I'd talked about it to anyone, other than Landon. And I told you some things I've never told him." He blew out a breath. "I guess my subconscious took over." He felt his eyes filling once again. "Morgan, I would never, ever intentionally do or say anything to hurt you."

Her hand rested gently on his cheek. "I know," she whispered. "Maybe you need more time. We've moved awfully fast."

Brandon frowned. "What? No, Morgan. I know that I love you."

"And I love you, Bran. But maybe your heart isn't fully healed yet."

He didn't know what to say to that. "Are you saying—" he could hardly bear to speak the words. "Do you want to take a step back? Take a break?"

"Not really. But maybe we should put the brakes on a bit

to let your heart catch up. We can see how things go at Thanksgiving," she said. "Maybe we should wait to tell our families. Let's pray about it and see what God says."

Brandon was ready to turn this over to God. "I think that's a fantastic idea." He took her hands. "Are we okay?" he whispered.

Morgan nodded. She looked tired, but he didn't think she was holding anything back.

He stood, and lifted her to her feet. "I need to get home," he said. "Can I bring my travel mug in for a fill-up?"

"Sure."

Brandon came back into the cabin and she filled the mug and handed it to him. He set it on the counter and opened his arms. He wanted to give her the choice.

She came right to him, and Brandon's heart lightened a bit. He held her and drew in a deep breath to memorize her essence. "I love you, Morgan," he whispered.

"I love you, too, Bran. Text me when you get home."

Brandon nodded.

34

AFTER BRANDON LEFT, Morgan sat by the fire and cried and had a long talk with God. She felt inadequate, and like she would never fill the space in Bran's heart that Darla once had. She didn't know how to be a mother, and could never give Bran a son, or the girls a brother or even a sister.

She spent some time in prayer, and opened her Bible. Her devotional for that day was eerily timely. It talked about how God's plans are better than our plans, and how desperately He wishes the very best for all of His children. Morgan also realized that with a surrendered heart, her hopes and dreams would change to be the ones that God wanted all along for her, instead of the other way around. Morgan couldn't pray enough prayers to change God's plan for her to something she concocted on her own, if it wasn't His best for her.

Morgan left for home a little after noon, filled with peace. She lifted her prayers to God and asked Him to heal Bran's heart, to show him His plan, and to lead both of them on whatever path He had for them.

She began counting the moments until she'd see Bran

again, and have five whole days with him and their families in Wisconsin.

35

"COME ON, GIRLS! You don't have to take every doll you own to Grandma and Grandpa's," Brandon called up the staircase. He looked at his watch. "Mor—Miss Morgy is going to be here any minute. Let's get a move on!" Since Morgan lived in the city, it made more sense for her to drive here and leave her car, since it was on the way. Brandon wanted to get on the road. It was a three-hour drive with no traffic, which certainly wasn't going to be the case the night before Thanksgiving.

Sara's voice came from just behind him. "I'm glad Morgan caught us before we left." She stepped around him and started up the stairs. "I'll get the girls. My bag's in the kitchen, ready to go."

Brandon ran a hand through his hair. *That's right. The Morgan's-having-car-trouble story.* They had talked a little on the phone and texted, but he hadn't seen her since he'd left the cabin on Sunday morning. With it being a short work week, both of them were extremely busy. He missed her terribly, but her suggestion to take their burden to the Lord in prayer had been a good one. Brandon didn't feel like he'd gotten an answer yet, but he felt like he was back on even footing with God again.

He rolled his eyes when he saw Sara's "bag." It was the size of a small vehicle, and even before he grabbed the handle, he knew it weighed as much. As he was wrestling it into the back of the SUV, he saw headlights, and Morgan pulled into the driveway. He'd left the right-side garage door up, and motioned her to pull in next to Sara's car.

Brandon trotted into the garage and opened Morgan's door. He glanced toward the door to the house and leaned in for a quick kiss. "Hey, babe," he whispered with a grin.

"Bran! Where are Sara and the girls?" Morgan was grinning, too.

"Inside. We're fine." He helped her out of the car. "I don't know how I'm going to spend three hours in a car with you and pretend that you're nothing more than Landon's sister-in-law." He grabbed her bag—which was more reasonably sized than Sara's—out of the trunk and rolled it to the SUV.

Just then, Sara and the girls came bursting out of the house. "Remember, your car was making a noise," he whispered to Morgan.

"Miss Morgy!" April and Shelbie squealed, and ran to her. Brandon's heart swelled as he watched Morgan hug them. Then he was busy with all the totes and bags that Sara pressed into his hands.

"What's all this stuff?"

"Things the girls and I need," his sister replied. "Hi, Morgan. Oh, your boots are so cute."

"Hi, Sara. Thanks."

"I hope your car trouble isn't anything serious."

"Umm, no, it's just making a rattle, but I didn't want to chance it."

"Well, I'm glad you can ride with us," Sara said. "Makes more sense anyway."

Brandon shook his head and moved things around in the back. "We're not going to Europe for a month, Peanut," he muttered. "You need to be more sensible, like Morgan."

"Whatever," she retorted. She and Morgan helped get the girls buckled in, and Morgan moved to climb in the back seat.

"You sit up front, Morgan," Sara said.

"Oh—you don't have to do that." Morgan glanced at Brandon.

"I want to. I'll probably fall asleep anyway." She clambered into the back seat and sat between her nieces.

"Well, let's get this show on the road," Brandon said. He and Morgan got in, and after a few more adjustments, they were off.

"Ah, I noticed the skis on top of the car," Morgan said. "Who's going skiing?"

"All of us, on Friday," Brandon said. "It's a family tradition."

"It's a blast," Sara called out. "Do you ski, Morgan?"

She shook her head. "No, I've never been. I guess I've just never wanted to."

Brandon wanted to take her hand and promise to help her learn, but instead he said, "We've gotten Kelsea on skis. It's easier than you think."

Morgan laughed. "I'd love to see that. I'm sure she won't go this year with the babies."

"St. Clairs are on skis before they can walk," Brandon said, and slid a smile her way.

"Darn right," Sara chimed in.

Morgan shook her head. "Well, I've brought plenty to do, so I can just stay at the house out of the way on Friday."

Brandon decided not to push it. He turned the radio on to get the traffic report and turned his attention to the road. Morgan chatted easily with the girls and Sara, and he was content to listen to them. Morgan fit so well into his life. He found himself anxious to come clean with their families about their relationship, but didn't want to run ahead of God. He was really looking forward to the long weekend and hoped that he and Morgan could sneak off for some time alone, but with all the people there, it wouldn't be easy.

Once they cleared the suburbs, the trip went by quickly, and when they were about an hour from his parents' house, the back seat went completely quiet. Brandon looked in his mirror. "Are they asleep?" he said softly to Morgan.

She turned around and looked. "Yes," she nodded. Brandon put his arm on the console between them and turned his hand, palm up. He looked at Morgan. *It's your choice, babe.* She smiled and laced her fingers with his. He squeezed her hand, and she squeezed back.

This is going to be the best Thanksgiving ever.

36

MORGAN WAS SO happy to be at Brandon's parents' home. As soon as they'd arrived, she'd slipped into the role of being simply Kelsea's sister. It was both exciting and a little scary to think that someday, she might be a true member of the St. Clair family, instead of a shirt-tail relative.

The house was a rambling, multi-level abode. Sara happily shared her room with Morgan, and Kelsea and Landon and the babies were camped out in the family room on the lower level. Brandon and the girls were in his and Landon's old room, and Morgan and Kelsea's mom, Beth, was in the room that had belonged to Reagan St. Clair many years ago.

It was tortuous to be there with Brandon and act as if he was just her sister's brother-in-law and someone whom she didn't know all that well. Morgan busied herself talking with Kelsea and helping with the babies—who had changed so much since last May. They had little personalities now. Morgan was amused that Rose was the spunkier of the two, and little Isaac was sweetly calm. The two sisters agreed that they had to make a way to get together more often.

Morgan also loved watching her mom interact with her grandchildren. Beth Anderson had waited a long time to be a grandma, and loved every minute of it. Morgan could just imagine her joy if she inherited two more instant granddaughters someday.

It was a busy day getting dinner ready, and Morgan was happy to help. Janice St. Clair had already communicated through Kelsea that she would love for Morgan to decorate the place cards, and had gathered all the supplies for that. Morgan had a great time doing it, and let April and Shelbie help.

Finally, all the food was ready and it was time to sit down at the large dining room table. Janice and Beth had set the cards out, and Brandon was directly across from Morgan. Everyone held hands, and Jim gave a beautiful blessing. Then they began passing the dishes and chattering.

"Honey, where's the hot mustard?" Jim called to his wife from his end of the table.

"Dad, you and your hot mustard!" Sara exclaimed. She rolled her eyes at Morgan. "He slathers it on everything."

Janice jumped up. "Oh, let me grab that right now." She scurried away and was back in seconds. She set the jar down in front of Jim, and he reached up and gave her lips a peck.

Shelbie was sitting next to her grandpa. "Why do you always kiss Grandma?" she asked. Everyone around the table laughed.

He grabbed his granddaughter's little hand. "Because I love her!"

"Ohhhhhh," Shelbie said, drawing the lone syllable out.

"Then Daddy must love Miss Morgy!" She took a bite of her roll and didn't notice that everyone else had stopped eating.

Morgan's heart began to pound, and her gaze flew to Brandon.

His amber eyes sparkled at her and then he smiled. "Well, babe, I think God just answered our prayer." Out of the corner of her eye, Morgan saw her mother's jaw drop, and Kelsea and Landon exchanged a triumphant look. Brandon laid down his napkin, stood, and walked around the table to her. Morgan rose and he took her hands.

Brandon looked at their family members, every one of whom was grinning from ear to ear. "Morgan and I have been together for over a month. We're still working through some things, but Shelbie's right." Then he stared into Morgan's eyes. "I'm very much in love with Morgan."

Morgan was oblivious to everything and everyone else in the room except this amazing man. Her smile felt a mile wide. "And I love Brandon with all my heart." And then he framed her face with his hands and kissed her, and everyone began to clap and cheer.

"I knew it!" Kelsea exclaimed. Her face was filled with joy.

"You did not!" Morgan exclaimed. She and Brandon wrapped their arms around one another, and she looked up at him. "Bran, I didn't tell."

Sara pointed at Kelsea. "You only knew because I knew first, and told you," she said in a sing-song voice.

"You did not!" Brandon rolled his eyes. "We kept it a secret."

"Well, obviously not from Shelbie!" Landon interjected.

Laughter raced around the room. Brandon kissed the top of Morgan's head and returned to his seat.

Sara set down her utensils. "If that's the best you two can keep a secret, you're in trouble." She tented her hands in front of her and looked around the table, no doubt to garner everyone's attention. Sara loved to entertain a crowd. "Whenever Morgan comes over, she finds an excuse to leave the room." She flicked a hand at her brother. "Then *he* leaves, and in a little while, *she* comes back—with swollen lips—and then *he* comes back—smelling like her perfume!"

Everyone laughed uproariously—even April and Shelbie, who didn't understand a thing. Morgan thought she and Brandon laughed the hardest.

"I saw you holding hands in the car last night," Sara added smugly.

Brandon looked at Morgan and shook his head. "She was faking being asleep," he said. "I should have known. She did that all the time when she was little."

"And," Sara said, "what about that rattle in your car, Morgan?"

Morgan felt her face heating up, and bit back a hysterical giggle. Brandon looked at his sister. "You think you're so smart, Peanut," he said with a grin.

"Bro, Kelsea and I knew," Landon said. "You started calling me with woman questions at the same time Morgan started calling Kelsea with guy questions."

Morgan and Brandon looked at each other, wide-eyed.

"Neither of you gave anything away about who you were dating," Kelsea said, "but we figured it out." She grinned at Morgan.

"And your stories didn't sync up exactly," Landon added with a twinkle in his eye.

Morgan and Brandon just stared at one another, smiling.

"Did all this begin last Mothers' Day at Kelsea and Landon's?" Beth asked.

Morgan and Brandon answered in unison. "Definitely not!" They burst out laughing, and everyone joined in.

"Sounds like there's a story there," Landon said.

When the laughter died down, Jim raised his glass. "To Brandon and Morgan, and whatever the Lord has in store for them."

"To Brandon and Morgan," everyone echoed, and clinked glasses. Brandon leaned across the table, touched his glass to Morgan's, and winked.

"I love you," he mouthed.

This is the best Thanksgiving ever.

37

AFTER DINNER, LANDON, Kelsea, Brandon, and Morgan offered to do all the clean-up since their moms had prepared most of the meal. Janice and Beth were happy to join Jim in the family room with all the children. Brandon couldn't wait to finish the chore so he could get Morgan out of there. Their kiss in the dining room in front of their families had been very circumspect. He had gone several days without a real kiss, and couldn't wait to get her alone.

He thought he was being helpful, but all he was really doing was trailing around after Morgan. She was working at the sink when Brandon came in with the rest of the glasses. He deposited them on the counter, wrapped his arms around her waist, and whispered in her ear. She giggled.

"Oh honestly, you two, get out of here," Kelsea said good-naturedly. "Landon and I will finish."

"You sure?" Brandon asked. He grabbed a towel and handed it to Morgan so she could dry her hands.

"Yes, we're sure," Landon said. "It's like being around two teenagers." He wiggled his eyebrows. "And if you leave, I can get a few moments alone with my wife."

Brandon didn't waste any time. He grabbed Morgan's hand and pulled her into the family room, where a Disney movie played on the large TV screen. "April and Shelbie, Miss Morgy and I are going for a walk. Be good until we get back," Brandon instructed.

"Bye, Daddy. Bye, Miss Morgy," April said. She was sitting in an overstuffed chair holding Isaac, supervised by Grandpa.

Shelbie stood and put her hands on her little hips. "Are you gonna kiss Miss Morgy again, Daddy?" she asked.

All the adults hooted with laughter. "You bet I am!" Brandon answered with a grin, and the laughter got even louder. He helped Morgan on with her coat, and ushered her out the door.

Holding hands, they walked down the long driveway and turned left when they got out to the road. After they had reached a more secluded spot, Brandon stopped under a tree and pulled her into his arms.

And kissed her with all the love in his heart.

He rested his forehead against hers. "I love you so much, Morgan."

"I love you more, Bran."

"Impossible!" He squeezed her until she squealed. Then he got serious. "Morgan, I've spent a lot of time with God since last weekend, and He's given me peace. And obviously, He answered our prayer tonight. A part of me will always love Darla, but I'm head over heels in love with you now, and ready to move forward."

"As long as I'm your present and future, that's all I need," Morgan whispered.

They kissed again, then walked, arm in arm. It was a

cold, clear night. The stars were out and there was a three-quarter moon. As they ambled along with the moonlight washing over them, Brandon had never felt so content and at peace.

"So, you called Kelsea for advice?" He smiled at Morgan so she'd know that he wasn't upset.

"And you called Landon?" she countered with a lilt in her voice.

"I didn't give him any clues," Brandon said. "What did you tell her?"

"Just that you were TDH and into sports."

He eyed her warily. "What's TDH?"

Morgan stopped and looped her hands around his neck. "Tall, dark, and handsome," she whispered, and pulled his head down for a kiss.

After a few moments, they resumed their walk.

"Are you ready for tomorrow?" he asked.

Morgan looked at him. "Don't tell me you're one of those people who goes to the mall at midnight to be the first in line when the stores open." She shook her head. "It sounds like something you would totally be into. Crowds and chaos."

He grimaced. "You know I'm not a shopper." They both laughed. "No, remember? We're all going skiing."

Morgan stopped walking. "Oh, I'd forgotten about that."

He leaned over and nuzzled her neck. "I'm going to teach you to ski."

"Bran, really, I—it won't work. I tried to ice skate once and it was a disaster. I have weak ankles."

He sighed. "Babe, skiing is completely different from ice skating."

Morgan twisted her hands in front of her. "I'm just such a klutz, Bran. I don't want to embarrass you in front of your family. Really, I'd rather stay at the house. I brought things to work on."

"Like what?"

"Knitting. And I have papers to grade."

Brandon couldn't believe what he was hearing. "*Knitting?* My grandma knits. That's for old ladies."

Morgan stopped walking. "It is not! I'm making scarves and hats and mittens for the girls for Christmas. A friend of mine spins and dyes her own yarn. They'll be one of a kind." She looked a little hurt, and Brandon felt badly for what he had said.

He pulled her into his arms and kissed her forehead. "I'm sorry. I shouldn't have said that. But especially now that you're my girlfriend, everyone will expect you to come skiing. You can't let life pass you by while you sit at the house painting or knitting or grading papers." He pulled her close and she let out a soft sigh. "For me?" he whispered, and kissed her in a way he knew that she loved.

When they came apart, she looked at him dreamily. "That's not fair, Bran, and you know it." He could tell she was teasing. "Okay, for you, I'll try."

38

"I TOLD YOU I couldn't ski!"

Morgan bit down on her lip to keep from screaming. Bran squatted next to her. He removed his gloves and ran his fingers expertly over her ankle, which was already beginning to swell.

"I don't think it's broken," he said. "But it's a bad sprain." He turned his head in Landon's direction. "We need to pack snow around it to try to minimize the swelling."

Morgan clamped her mouth shut. She was so embarrassed. Even April and Shelbie were naturals on skis. She was so cold, and now they were packing snow around her lower leg, ankle, and foot. Kelsea took her scarf off and handed it to Brandon, and he wrapped it around the snow pack. Then he stood.

Landon motioned to Kelsea. "We'll get you up, Morgan." In one swift movement, they did that, and Bran scooped her up in his arms and walked across the slope to a far-off spot where Jim had brought Brandon's SUV as close as he could get it. Morgan buried her face in his neck and cried.

Kelsea ran to catch up with them. "I'm coming, too, Morgy." She opened the back door and Jim and Brandon got her situated in the back seat.

Morgan grabbed the collar of Brandon's coat. "Are we going home?" she said through her tears.

"No, I want to get an x-ray to be sure," he said. He leaned in and kissed her cheek. "I'm sorry, Morgan. I'm really sorry."

She nodded but didn't say anything.

"I'll be with you every minute," Brandon said. He ran around to the other side and got in, and tenderly put her injured foot in his lap. Kelsea and Jim got into the front seat, and Jim drove them to the hospital. It felt like an eternity to get there, but the trip only took about twenty minutes.

From the moment they got in the ER, Dr. St. Clair took charge. If Morgan hadn't been so miserable, she would have been impressed and swooning over his commanding presence. Once they got some pain medication into her, she began to relax. Bran kept his promise and never left her side.

The x-ray showed a bad sprain, just as he had predicted, and Morgan's foot was tightly bound. An hour later, they left with more pain meds, bandages, and a pair of crutches. Bran got her settled in the back seat with her foot propped up on some wadded-up blankets. Then he went around and slipped in next to her and took her in his arms.

As his father drove them home, Bran held her close and whispered in her ear, "Babe, I'm so, so sorry. I shouldn't have pushed you to do something you didn't want to do."

"I don't know how I'm going to get through the end of the semester," she said softly through her tears. "I have so much going on. I'm not even going to be able to get around. Those crutches will be a nightmare with the snow and ice we already have on the ground. And I won't be able to drive. And my bedroom and bath are on the second floor." Her pain-filled mind was swimming with unsettling thoughts.

"We'll figure it out together, Morgan, I promise," Brandon said, stroking her hair.

When they got back to the St. Clair's house, everyone was waiting for them. Brandon carried Morgan in and took her straight upstairs to Sara's room. "Sara, can you sleep with the girls tonight?" he asked his sister. Morgan looked at him with surprise. He laid her down on the bed. "I'll make a bed on the floor."

"Bran, you can't sleep on the floor," Morgan said.

"I'm not leaving you," he said. He looked at Beth and Janice who had come into the room with everything the hospital had sent home. "Mom, could you get some more pillows and blankets?"

"Of course," Janice said and hurried away.

"Morgan, would you like some tea, or cocoa?" her mother asked. "Something to eat?"

Morgan nodded. "They gave me some crackers at the hospital, and they said the pain medication might make me nauseous on an empty stomach."

Janice came back into the room, her arms laden. "How about some soup?" she asked.

"That sounds good," Morgan nodded.

Brandon squeezed her hand. "Mom makes the best vegetable barley soup and homemade bread," he said. "It's part of our Friday-after-Thanksgiving tradition." He and Beth took the pillows and blankets and got Morgan situated.

"I'll go help Janice," Beth said. She planted a kiss on Morgan's head.

"Thanks so much, Mom," Morgan said.

Brandon sat down gingerly next to her and took her hand. "I love you, Morgan. I'll stay with you every moment." He kissed her tenderly, and Morgan's heart melted.

She touched the side of his face. "I'm so lucky to have you," she whispered.

Kelsea appeared at the door. April and Shelbie were each holding one of her hands. "Are you up for some company, Miss Morgy? The girls are a little worried about you."

Bran scooted away from her a little. "Of course," Morgan said, holding out her hands. "Come on in, girls."

"Just be careful not to bump Miss Morgy's leg," Brandon said.

April and Shelbie stood by the side of the bed and took her hands. "I'm sorry you got hurt, Miss Morgy," April said.

"Does it hurt bad?" Shelbie asked.

Morgan didn't want to scare them. "It hurts a little, but I took some medicine and it feels better." The girls stayed for another few minutes and then went with Kelsea, promising to make some pictures for Morgan to help her feel better.

"They're so precious," Morgan murmured after they had left.

Bran's amber eyes were tender. "They already love you," he whispered.

After that, her mother came in with a tray with soup and bread. Morgan didn't think she was hungry, but finished every bite, and then fell asleep with Bran holding her hand.

They drove back to Chicago Sunday morning, and by that time Morgan was feeling much better. When they got to

Bran's house, there was a large box waiting for them. Somehow, he had come up with a little battery-powered scooter on which she could rest the knee of her injured leg and motor along. She thought it was ingenious, and was relieved that it would make it possible to get around campus.

Bran carried her into the house and laid her gently on the couch, and Sara brought some pillows and an ice pack for her ankle. Bran knelt by her side and took her hand. "We want you to stay here and let us take care of you."

"We have it all figured out," Sara said. "You can stay in my apartment and I'll sleep upstairs. There are like twelve empty bedrooms up there," she quipped, and Morgan smiled. Sara held out her hand. "Give me your condo keys, and text me everything you need."

"I still can't drive," Morgan said. "I guess I can take the Metra to work from here."

Brandon shook his head. "No way. Sara and I will take you to campus and your sessions and pick you up."

Morgan couldn't believe it. She shook her head in disbelief.

"Give up, Morgan, you're outnumbered," Sara said with a smile. Morgan got her keys out of her purse and handed them to Sara.

"I'll take the girls with me, if that's okay," she said. Brandon looked at Morgan and she nodded. "They'll love helping, and it will give you two some time alone." Sara wiggled her eyebrows and left with a wave.

"She's really something," Morgan said. "She's terrific."

"Yeah, she is," Brandon said, and leaned in to kiss her. "Isn't this better than going home?" He kissed her again. "We'll practically be living together." Another, longer kiss.

Morgan giggled. "With three chaperones," she said. But she was so relieved to have someone taking care of her. It felt like family. Maybe, just maybe...

"I love you, Morgan," Bran whispered.

39

THEY FELL INTO an easy routine over the next week. Brandon loved seeing Morgan at the start and end of each day, and he could tell that the girls loved it, too. She completely fit in with them, and he was becoming more and more convinced that they had a solid chance at a future together.

The night before she went home, after the girls had gone to bed, Morgan asked if they could talk. They sat down by the fire and Brandon thought that he could spend every night for the rest of his life like this.

"There's something I need to tell you," she said. "I don't know exactly how to say it."

Brandon tried to think of anything he'd done wrong, or said, that could cause Morgan to look so serious. He took her hand. "You can talk to me about anything, Morgan, you know that."

To his relief, she smiled at him. "I know, but I don't want you to get the wrong idea."

"You let me be the judge of that," he said, and squeezed her hand.

And then she started talking about her infertility issues and her deep desire to foster or adopt one or more children. Morgan's beautiful features came to life when she talked about some of the children in the arts program who had captured her heart, and how she wanted to give them a loving and safe environment. "I know we haven't talked specifically about our future, and I'm not trying to force that conversation," she said. "But this is so important to me, and I just thought I should tell you how I felt."

He raised her hand to his lips and kissed it. "I'm glad you shared it with me," he said. "We already agreed that there are lots of ways to grow a family, and I'm completely in agreement with you." They sat by the fire for a long time and talked about their childhoods, growing up, and what Morgan's family felt like after her father died. Brandon was more in love with her than ever.

Morgan went back to her condo the next Sunday night. She told Brandon that she needed to get through the last two weeks of her semester without distractions, and kissed him goodbye and whispered in his ear that she loved the way he distracted her.

Brandon was busy at work, too, and suddenly, it was December 23. They had Christmas with Sara before she drove home to Wisconsin for two weeks. Morgan had given her a silk scarf that she had painted herself, and Sara gave Morgan a beautiful pair of earrings. Brandon was grateful that there was a strong bond between them.

Then it was his birthday, Christmas Eve, and they packed up April and Shelbie and drove to Beth's house in Kankakee.

It was cold but clear and sunny, and it felt entirely natural to be in the car with his girls in the backseat and Morgan by his side, holding his hand.

"Are we going to Unca Landon and Aunt Kelsea's house?" Shelbie called out.

"No, remember, we're going to Grandma Beth's house," Brandon answered. He squeezed Morgan's hand. They had agreed at Thanksgiving that the girls could call her that since she was their little cousins' grandma.

"Yay!" the girls shouted.

"I love Grandma Beth!" Shelbie said.

"She's fun," April added.

Kelsea and Landon and the twins were already there when they arrived mid-afternoon. They'd gotten several inches of fresh snow overnight, and there was a festive air in the house. He and Morgan had shipped a box to Beth full of gifts for April and Shelbie from "Santa," and Brandon looked forward to wrapping those with Morgan tonight after the girls had gone to bed.

After they got all their gifts and suitcases inside, the girls went with Grandma Beth to read a story to the twins and get them down for a nap. Brandon joined Morgan, Landon, and Kelsea in the family room.

Brandon loved seeing the home where Morgan had grown up. He was instantly drawn to the wall where hers and Kelsea's growing-up pictures were displayed. "Weren't you the cutest little girl?" he teased. He stopped at a photo of the family taken out on the front steps of the house. It was obvious that Morgan looked like her dad.

She came and stood next to him. "This is the last picture of the four of us," Morgan said softly.

Brandon put his arms around her and held her. "What was his name?"

"Andrew. He went by Andy. He was the best dad, so much fun."

Brandon kept looking at the pictures. "Oh, this is a great one!" he burst out laughing, and Morgan giggled.

Kelsea piped up. "I don't even have to ask which one you're laughing at. My eighth grade graduation." In the picture, Kelsea was dressed in black pants and a top, her arms crossed in front of her and one hip jutted out in a defiant pose. Her long, dark hair hung limply on each side of her face, and she scowled at the camera. It looked like she was wearing scruffy, black tennis shoes. Morgan stood next to her in total contrast. Her golden hair was curled and pulled back with a headband, and she wore a pale blue dress with a flowered scarf, and white sandals with a matching purse. She stood proud and tall and smiled for the camera as if she were on Hollywood's red carpet.

"You had a flair for fashion even back then, babe," Brandon said, giving her a squeeze.

"I was so mad that Mom refused to let me wear jeans," Kelsea said. "I was supposed to change out of those tennis shoes, too, but I think she was too worn out over the battle to push it."

Landon grinned at his wife and took her hand. "I can't wait until Rose Elizabeth gets to be that age. What goes around comes around." They all laughed.

Just then, April and Shelbie burst into the room. "Grandma Beth said we could build a snowman!" Shelbie shouted.

"Shh!" April scolded. "You'll wake the babies."

"Grandma Beth said we could build a snowman!" Shelbie repeated in a stage whisper.

Beth followed them, holding two pairs of snow pants. "They got these out of their suitcase. I said they had to ask you, Brandon."

He smiled. "It's fine with me." He looked at Morgan. "Do you mind if I go outside with them?"

She shook her head. "Not at all."

"Actually, I'd love to go with them," Beth said. "You stay in here where it's warm and relax."

"If you're sure," Brandon said.

"I'm sure," Beth said with a smile. "Oh, girls," she said to Kelsea and Morgan, "could you finish putting the lasagna together, and make up the salad?"

"Sure thing, Mom," the sisters answered in unison. Beth followed April and Shelbie out of the room.

"Mmm, sounds good," Brandon said.

"It's our traditional Christmas Eve meal," Morgan said. "We'll have turkey with all the trimmings tomorrow."

Kelsea looked at Morgan. "Mom couldn't wait for the girls to get here. I think she was more excited about them coming than you."

Morgan laughed. "I know she's happy to have little ones in the house for Christmas. It makes it more fun for everyone." She stood. "Come on, Sissy, let's get to it." They went into the kitchen and the two brothers sat and chatted for a while about inconsequential things.

Brandon got up and went into the dining room to look out the front window and check on the girls, and Landon followed him. April and Shelbie's faces were flushed with joy, so different from last year's Christmas that had been drenched with grief. He felt his brother's gaze on him. "I'm really glad we're here," Brandon murmured.

Landon smiled. "I can't believe how much your life has changed just since last May when you visited us in St. Louis."

Brandon raised an eyebrow. "Yeah, the new job was a game-changer." But he knew what Landon was really getting at, and let out a breath. "I'm ready to move on, and I want to spend the rest of my life with her."

"You giving her a ring tomorrow?" Landon asked.

"No," Brandon replied, "I'm thinking Valentine's Day."

"That's great, man," Landon said, and reached out to squeeze his brother's shoulder. "I'm really happy for you."

Brandon hesitated. He didn't want to betray Morgan's confidence if Landon didn't already know about her infertility issues, but he wanted Landon to know. He lowered his voice. "She—we probably won't be able to have children of our own," he said, "but we've talked about how great we think fostering and adopting are. We're completely in sync about that."

Landon nodded. One glance between the brothers told Brandon everything. "I can't wait to see what God has in store for you," Landon said.

"Me, too," Brandon said with a grin.

Kelsea called from the kitchen, "you guys want some Christmas cider?" Brandon correctly guessed that this was the source of the enticing aromas of cinnamon and clove. When he and Landon got into the kitchen, he pulled Morgan around a corner where they could have a moment of privacy.

"I just had a conversation with Landon," he whispered,

"and, well, I mentioned your infertility issues, just in a general way. It just sort of came up. I hope I wasn't breaking confidence."

"Bran, it's okay," she answered. "He knows. It all began back when he and Kelsea met and were married."

"I would never—"

She silenced him with a finger to his lips. "Bran, I know." She smiled. "Let's go get some cider."

They went back into the kitchen, and Brandon sat on one of the bar stools at the counter. Morgan came and perched against his knee, and their arms automatically went around one another.

Landon set down mugs of cider for them, and Kelsea began putting the food they'd prepared for dinner into the fridge. "You want some help, Sissy?" Morgan asked.

"Don't worry, I've got it." She raised an eyebrow. "It doesn't look like you and Dr. Moron could bear to be more than an inch apart from each other, anyway."

Brandon felt Morgan blanch, and make a sound in her throat.

"Oh, whoopsie!" Kelsea said, and she and Morgan began to laugh.

Morgan covered her mouth as a hysterical giggle escaped. She laid a hand on Brandon's shoulder. "Bran, I'm so sorry. That's what I called you in my head the weekend we met at Kelsea and Landon's!"

He threw back his head and laughed, and heard Landon's laughter join his. He pulled Morgan close. "I *was* a moron that weekend."

"I'll bet you've been called worse at the hospital, bro," Landon said with a grin.

"I *know* I have," Brandon said. He planted a kiss near Morgan's ear. "I love you, babe," he whispered.

The family went to church together for the five o'clock Christmas Eve service, and Brandon's heart was full. April and Shelbie wore their pretty new Christmas dresses from Grandma and Grandpa St. Clair. Then they all came back to the house for the delicious Italian dinner, after which Beth and Morgan brought out a birthday cake and ice cream. Everyone sang and Brandon blew out the candles. He already knew what he was going to wish for, and looked right at Morgan when he did it. Her gorgeous green eyes sparkled at him in the candlelight.

Then he opened his gifts. The St. Clair family had always recognized Brandon's birthday apart from Christmas, and made sure that the celebration was memorable. Brandon was filled with gratitude and touched by everyone's generosity. There were gifts from Landon and Kelsea, Beth, and the girls. April and Shelbie were excited and proud of the paperweights they had made him, and he promised to put them on his desk at work. Brandon loved the small framed silhouette portraits of them that Sara had arranged.

"Here's one more," Morgan said. She held up a long tube wrapped in white tissue paper and tied with a pink ribbon on one end and a purple one on the other.

"Open it, Daddy! Open it!" the girls squealed.

Brandon extended his arms and held the tube lengthwise in front of him. "I think I need some help. Each of you can untie a ribbon."

"I get the purple one!" Shelbie said, hopping up and

down. They did as he instructed, and helped him get the paper off, then he carefully pulled out a large sheet of paper and unrolled it.

"What is it, Daddy?" Shelbie clapped her little hands.

"It's us!" April exclaimed.

"Oh, Morgan," Brandon breathed. It was an incredible pencil drawing of the girls in an outdoor setting. It looked a little like their backyard. In the picture, April sat cross-legged on the grass, picking petals off a flower, looking serene and thoughtful. Shelbie was trying to catch a butterfly that was just out of her reach, her little face filled with joy and wonder. It was a black-and-white sketch, except for the flower, which was pink, and the butterfly, which was shades of purple.

Brandon didn't have the first clue how Morgan had captured the essence of his daughters so perfectly. He would treasure this gift forever. He felt a lump in his throat. "This is so beautiful, babe, thank you."

"You're welcome," Morgan replied. "I'll have it framed when we get home."

Brandon passed the picture for Kelsea, Landon, and Beth to look at. "Wow, that's amazing," Landon said. "I have no artistic talent whatsoever."

"Morgan, you outdid yourself on this one," Beth said, her face beaming with pride.

"This is one of your best, Morgy," Kelsea agreed. "Would you do a sketch of Rose and Isaac?"

Brandon exchanged a glance with Morgan. "Why don't you wait until tomorrow, Kelsea?" he said.

Kelsea clapped her hands. "Ooh, I can't wait!" she exclaimed.

Brandon held out his arm to Morgan. "Come here," he said. "Thank you," he whispered when she got close enough, and then he kissed her.

"Happy Birthday, Bran," she whispered back.

"Daddy, you *always* kiss Miss Morgy!" Shelbie exclaimed.

"Yes, I sure do," Brandon said. His heart was so full. *Best birthday ever.*

40

MORGAN HAD SPENT many Christmases in this house, but none compared to this one. She looked around the chaos that reigned in her mother's family room, and her heart felt steeped in joy. The house was filled with laughter and love. Christmas wrapping paper and ribbons were everywhere, despite her mother's attempt to gather them up after each gift had been opened. The babies weren't walking yet, but they were scooting around and putting everything in their mouths. April and Shelbie were excited about everything and were great little helpers. Everyone loved their homemade Christmas gifts from Morgan, and she was relieved that the sweater she made for Bran fit him perfectly. It was the best Christmas Morgan could remember.

She sat on the floor with her back against the couch. Bran sat next to her.

"Here's the last one," he said, handing her a slim, flat box about eight inches square. Morgan had been holding her breath, wondering if he might give her an engagement ring. The prospect both thrilled and scared her.

"Should I try to guess what it is?" Morgan said, giving the box a shake. It was very light, and didn't make any noise.

"Betcha can't," he replied with a lazy smile.

She unwrapped the box to reveal a thick cream linen envelope lined in gold foil, and was more intrigued than ever. When she opened it, her heart leapt into her throat. "You're—you can't be serious," she said. "Bran!"

"What is it?" Kelsea asked.

"Tickets to an exhibit at the Palomino Gallery in New York in February," Morgan said. Her heart beat erratically.

"I'm guessing that's some kind of artist," Landon said.

"Only the most incredible post-impressionist artist of the twentieth century!" Morgan exclaimed. "Bran, how did you—I can't believe—"

He laughed. "Well, full disclosure—I had help from Juanita Ross." He looked at the others. "Morgan's colleague," he clarified. "I asked her about getting you a painting or taking you to an art event, and she told me this artist, Angelina Palomino, was one of your favorites, and the name rang a bell."

"Jacko Palomino, the Bears' linebacker," Landon interjected.

"Bingo," Brandon nodded. "Angelina is his sister. One phone call, and I had these tickets."

Morgan cupped his chin in her hand and kissed him. "Bran, this is an amazing gift. Thank you so much."

He put his arm around her. "There's two tickets. Okay if I tag along?"

A romantic weekend in New York with him? That was a big step. Morgan couldn't believe it. "Of course," she whispered.

He kissed her cheek. "Merry Christmas, Morgan."

"Merry Christmas, Bran."

It was Christmas night. All the kids were in bed. Landon and Kelsea had gone for a walk, Beth was somewhere else in the house, and Morgan and Brandon were cuddling on the couch in the living room.

He and the girls were driving to his parents' in Wisconsin tomorrow afternoon to have Christmas with them, and Morgan would take the train back to Chicago in a couple of days. Bran was planning to arrive home on December 30.

"Let's talk about New Year's Eve," he said.

Morgan had been thinking about it. She hoped for a quiet, romantic night alone. Sara would still be in Wisconsin and Morgan knew Brandon wouldn't want to leave the girls. She thought they could stay in, make homemade pizzas, then do a craft or play games with the girls and put them down early. "All right," Morgan replied. "What do you usually like to do?"

"Well, I usually like going out on New Year's Eve, but last year I didn't do anything," Brandon shrugged. "I stayed home with the girls and was in bed by ten." Then he perked up. "But the Center is renting out the Allegra for the night. I have to be there, and I want you to go with me so I can show you off to everyone." He kissed Morgan on the sensitive spot on her neck.

She squirmed away from him. "Bran, I, um, wow. The Allegra." She knew it was one of Chicago's trendiest nightclubs, even though she'd never set foot in it. "I don't think I even have anything fancy enough to wear."

"Me, either. But I'm renting a tux. You could probably rent a dress. Giselle told me she's doing that."

Morgan liked his assistant. "Is it going to be a big event?"

He nodded. "They're expecting about six hundred people, a lot of managers and coaches and players and their wives and girlfriends. It's one of those seen-and-be-seen things. I have to be there."

"What about the girls?"

He shrugged. "I'll hire a sitter. Sara gave me a couple of names."

Morgan frowned and twisted her hands in her lap. "Bran, I just—I'm not comfortable in big crowds. Especially celebrities and people like that. I'd feel so out of place."

He ruffled a hand through his hair. "Well, that's the circle I travel in now. They're really just people, like anyone else." He pulled her closer. "You'll be on my arm all night. I'll never leave your side." He lowered his voice to a whisper. "Morgan, I can't go there alone. I need you there with me." He put his hands on either side of her face and kissed her once, twice, then slid his arms around her and deepened the kiss.

Morgan kissed him back and all her doubts vanished for a few moments. She told herself this wasn't a good idea, but couldn't resist him. "Are you trying to kiss me into saying yes?" she said as his lips trailed along her jawline and neck.

He laughed softly. "Maybe. Is it working?"

Morgan sighed. "Yes."

41

BRANDON RANG THE doorbell and waited for Morgan to answer. When she did, he wasn't prepared for what he saw.

She was utterly gorgeous. He whistled long and low. "Oh, wow, babe." He stepped in and closed the door. She wore a beautiful deep purple gown, high, silver pumps, and matching jewelry.

Brandon took her in his arms and slowly danced her around in a small circle. "You'll be the most beautiful woman there," he whispered. In her tall heels, she was closer than usual, and he took advantage with a long, slow kiss.

"Renting this dress was a great idea. I'll have to remember to thank Giselle. It really wasn't that expensive." She fingered his bow tie. "You look amazing, Bran," she said. She wore the silver bracelet he'd given her for her birthday.

"Your hair is beautiful." It was gathered into a knot at the nape of her neck. Brandon reached out and gently turned her so he could touch a golden curl.

"It's a chignon," she said. "Thank you."

He kissed her again. "Thank you for coming with me," he whispered when they came apart. "I love you."

"I love you, too."

In the car, he told her about all the people he thought would be there. She hadn't heard of most of them, even the biggest names. Sometimes, she would gaze at him with a deer-in-the-headlights look, and he would squeeze her hand. "Morgan, I'll be by your side the whole time. It'll be fine."

When they stepped into the club, Brandon laced his fingers with Morgan's, and she held on tight. They were immediately swept into the crowded, noisy, jubilant crowd. Brandon began making the rounds, trading back slaps with the men and bowing over the women's hands. He proudly introduced Morgan to everyone, and was so happy to have her there with him.

They spent the next hour moving through the room. Brandon felt as comfortable here as he did in the surgical theater. He loved the electricity in the room and enjoyed talking with people. He even met a few superstar athletes that he didn't know, yet. This evening was going to pay dividends for his career.

At one point when the crowd was packed tight, a woman with bright red hair wearing a short, skintight sequined copper dress slid by them. She gave a little finger wave and smiled up at Brandon. "Good evening, Dr. St. Clair," she cooed, and moved on.

"Who was that?" Morgan whispered.

He frowned. "I'm not sure. She might work in the Cubs' front office."

A waiter approached them with a tray. "Champagne?" he asked.

"Ah—no, thanks," Brandon replied. "Can we get some water?"

The waiter indicated a station with a silver carafe. Brandon led Morgan there and got each them a glass. "Do you want to go to the buffet now?"

She nodded. They filled their plates and found two seats at a round table. When they were finished, Brandon stood and held out his hand. "I need to make the rounds again." He pulled her close and kissed her temple. "You're doing great, babe."

42

MORGAN CLOSED THE bathroom stall door and let out a sigh. She didn't need to use the facilities, but she sat anyway. She just couldn't stand it one more minute. She had to get away.

Morgan rubbed her temples. The absence of noise should have been calming, but it wasn't. She was so out of her element. The constant movement, the press and heat of the crowd, the flashing lights, the loud music with its bone-rattling bass, all of it unnerved her. She felt like her smile was plastered on her face, and thought everyone else looked that way, too. None of it felt sincere. It was obvious to Morgan that the women were trying to outdo each other. She wished she had been brave enough to stay home and let Brandon come without her.

She heard the click of heels on the tile floor. "I just need to fix my makeup," a female voice said. "Brandon St. Clair is the hottest man *ever* in a tux! Did you see his mousy girlfriend?" Morgan peeked through the crack between the side of the stall. It was the redhead in the shimmering copper dress. She stood at the sink next to another woman.

"I heard she's an artist or something," the second woman said.

"Ugh," said Miss Copper. "Why would he want to be with someone like that? I heard that he's really into extreme sports and all kinds of exciting things. I can think of one extreme sport I'd like to do with him," she purred. There was no mistaking her meaning. Morgan cringed.

"Well, he looks pretty happy with her. If he's seriously involved with someone, give it up, Sheba," the second woman said.

Miss Copper put on a heavy coat of bright red lipstick and pouted at herself in the mirror. "Hey, they're all fair game until they're married. You know my motto. Whatever Sheba wants, Sheba gets. And Sheba wants that rich, sexy doctor. Come on, let's go. I am ready to par-tay!" Morgan waited until she'd heard the doors close and their footsteps had faded away.

She stepped out of the stall and looked at the woman in the mirror. Compared to most of the women out there, Morgan looked and felt like a wet dishrag. She shook her head slowly. *Why would he want to be with you?*

Morgan looked at her phone. It was only a little after ten. She couldn't believe they'd only been here two hours. It felt like two days. She steeled herself and returned to the party. It felt louder than when she'd left just ten minutes ago, but with the way the alcohol was flowing, she shouldn't have been surprised.

It took her almost another ten minutes to locate Brandon, chatting up a noisy group, and she leaned against him with relief. He slid his arm around her. "You okay?" he murmured into her ear.

She took a deep breath and shook her head. He looked into her eyes with surprise. "Are you sick, Morgan?"

"I just—the noise and everything, it's too much," she said. He looked like he didn't know what to say.

"I can—I'll just call an Uber and go home," she said.

"What? No, absolutely not, Morgan," he said sharply.

She almost burst into tears. "I need to go, Bran. I'm sorry."

He nodded. "All right." He looked around and took her hand. "I just have to say goodnight to a couple of folks."

Twenty minutes later, they finally left. Neither one of them said much in the car. When they pulled up in front of her condo, she turned to him. "I'm sorry, Bran."

"It's okay." He opened his arms. "Come here." He held her and kissed her forehead. "Can I come in?" She nodded.

Morgan was so happy to be back in her quiet, serene home. She laid her purse and keys on the hall table and turned to Brandon. Before she could apologize again, he kissed her tenderly. Then he took her hand and led her to the couch.

"I don't know what came over me," Brandon said, and he squeezed her hand. "I'd rather be here with you, Morgan. Honestly, I would. But I love crowds and excitement and noise. It invigorates me." He kissed her again. "Do you want me to turn the fireplace on?" She nodded.

He did that, then removed his jacket and sat. Morgan curled up next to him and laid her head on his chest. "I get my energy from the quiet," she said. "I know that doesn't make sense, but it does, to me." They sat and talked for over an hour and took kissing breaks, and then Brandon stood and raised her to her feet.

"It's almost midnight," he whispered, and they watched the last minutes of the year tick away on the clock over her mantel. At exactly midnight, he kissed her with a depth of passion yet unknown to Morgan, and all her doubts melted away.

"I love you, Dr. Morgan Anderson," Brandon said as he smiled into her eyes. "And I hope that we're together just like this at midnight on New Year's Eve for many, many years to come."

43

THE NEXT TWO weeks flew by. Morgan was busy preparing for the next semester, which would begin the third week of January. Brandon had one scheduled trip and two unscheduled ones, and she had hardly seen him. It looked like they were both free this Saturday, and she hoped they could spend some time with the girls, and then some time together, just the two of them.

He called her Friday night. "Hey babe, I'm on the plane coming home from Seattle."

Morgan's heart took wing. "When will you be home?" she asked.

"Not until about one in the morning."

"Can we get together this weekend? I miss you."

"Absolutely. That's one reason I was calling. How would you like to go skydiving tomorrow?"

Morgan was horrified. "Skydiving?"

"Yeah, one of the Cubs players has a timeshare plane, and is taking a group skydiving tomorrow. He invited me to come and bring a guest."

"Oh, Bran, I can't. I could never do that."

She heard him sigh. "Morgan, you're going to miss out on life if you don't try new things."

That got her hackles up. She'd tried skiing, and look how that turned out. "Brandon, I try new things all the time, and my life is just fine. I just don't happen to want to jump out of an airplane. And isn't that a pretty dangerous thing for a father with young children to be doing?"

He sighed again. "It's probably safer than driving on the Kennedy during rush hour. Dar and I used to do fun things all the time, even after the girls were born."

Morgan felt a sting as if he had slapped her. "Well, I'm not Dar!" she exclaimed.

"Sweetheart, that's not the point," he said. Neither of them said anything for a moment. "Morgan, I don't want to pass up this chance. There will be people there I need to meet. Will you come with me, or not?"

"No, Bran, I won't," she said firmly. Then she softened her voice. "But can we do something with the girls Saturday night?"

He sounded resigned. "Yeah, I'll call you when I get home tomorrow afternoon."

"I'll plan everything for tomorrow night. You won't have to do a thing." She paused. "I love you, Bran."

"I love you, too," he said, and disconnected.

44

WHEN THEY'D FINISHED the skydive and gotten back to the airport, Brandon had a text from Morgan. He looked at the time. *Perfect.* She was already at his house. She'd gone over early so Sara could spend the rest of the day and evening with friends. *On my way, I love you,* he texted her back.

When he got home and went through the kitchen door, Morgan was standing at the stove and the girls were at the counter doing something with tissue paper and scissors and glue and a bunch of other little messy things.

"Hi, Daddy!" they screamed. He kissed each of them on the head.

"We're making stained glass," Shelbie said.

"Those are awesome," he said. Then he went to Morgan and kissed her. "Mmm, what do you taste like?"

She pointed at the pot on the stove. "Homemade spaghetti sauce," she said. "I'm trying," she said with a laugh. Morgan held out the spoon to him, and he tasted it.

"Yum, it's good," he said. He kissed her again. "But you taste better."

She put the spoon down and ran her hands over his shoulders. "Thank you."

He put his hands on her waist and smiled at her. "I like coming home and seeing you and the girls here in the kitchen."

Morgan swallowed and nodded.

"Hey," he said. "Let me go up and change, and then I'll be back and we'll have pasgetti, right, girls?"

"Right, Daddy!" they said with glee.

He kissed Morgan's cheek. "And I'll tell you all about my day. It was incredible!"

Brandon took a quick shower, changed, and went back downstairs. Morgan was putting the finishing touches on dinner, and the girls were setting the table. He helped Morgan get the food, then they sat and held hands and he prayed for the meal.

Brandon loved this. It felt like a real home. It felt like family. He was hungry and eagerly took his first bite. And chewed. And chewed some more.

"Is it okay, Bran?" Morgan asked. She nibbled on her lip in a way that signaled to him that she was nervous.

"It's delicious! That's why I'm not talking, I'm too busy enjoying it."

"It's sooooooo good! I love pasgetti!" Shelbie exclaimed.

April nodded. "Me, too. I've never had crunchy pasgetti."

Morgan's face fell and she looked like was going to cry. She laid down her fork. "I didn't cook the noodles long enough."

Brandon leaned over and kissed her on the cheek.

"You'll get it next time. The sauce is amazing, babe. And it's not about the food. It's about being here, sharing a meal together." *As a family,* he almost added.

She squeezed his hand and gave him a tremulous smile, and Brandon felt like the sun had come out. After Thanksgiving, his birthday, and Christmas, he thought that it was time to have a serious talk about their future. He was thinking about proposing during their trip to New York next month.

"Who wants to hear about Daddy jumping out of an airplane?" he said.

"Me, me, me!" Shelbie squealed.

April's eyes got wide and she looked at Morgan. "I would be so scared!"

"Me, too!" Morgan replied.

So Brandon told them about the whole day and how exhilarating and fun it was, and what it felt like and looked like floating down from the sky. At one point he made a reference to his jumping buddy, Sheba.

"Who's Sheba, Daddy?" Shelbie said.

"She's one of the ladies who works for the Cubs," Brandon said. "She came by herself and so did I, so they put us together."

He noticed after that, Morgan got very quiet, but he didn't think anything of it. They finished dinner and Brandon tidied up the kitchen while Morgan helped the girls finish up their projects and clean everything up.

After they got the girls ready for bed, read books and said prayers with them, he and Morgan went back downstairs. The fireplace was going in the family room, and Brandon busied himself putting some soft music on. When he turned around, he was shocked to see Morgan standing there in her coat.

"Babe, what are you doing?"

"I'm going home, Bran. It was a long week, and I'm tired."

"I thought—I thought we would have some quiet time together. Just you and me. The way you like."

She sighed and looked away from him. "No, I need to go."

He went right to her and put his hands on her arms. "Morgan, what's wrong?"

Her eyes filled with tears, but she didn't say anything.

Brandon wrapped his arms around her and rubbed his hands over her back. "Come on, babe," he murmured. "Come sit with me and tell me what's wrong, and we'll figure it out together."

She let out a sigh and stood limply while he removed her coat, and he took her hand and led her to the couch. Brandon knew enough not to say anything, to let her talk first. He wrapped one arm around her and they sat there for several minutes with the soft music swirling around them.

Finally, she spoke. "Bran, I think it's time for us to talk about our future."

It was like she knew exactly what she was thinking! He took her hand and kissed it. "I was thinking the same thing."

"I'm not sure that this is going to work," she said.

Brandon's heart stopped. "Morgan, what do you mean? I thought—I love you! And you love me. What doesn't work?"

She swiped at her eyes, and Brandon quickly got up and grabbed some tissues from the kitchen counter. He sat next to her again and pressed them into her hand.

Her gorgeous green eyes were shiny with tears, and filled with pain. "We're so different," she said.

"Well, opposites attract," he said.

"But a couple needs to have a certain amount of things in common for it to work."

"I thought we did," he said quietly.

"Think about it, Bran. At our very core, we're totally different people. You're extroverted, I'm introverted. You're a city boy. I yearn for the country. You look at a picture of a river and think about white water rafting. I look at it and think about painting it." She paused. "The term *concert* means something entirely different to each of us."

Brandon took her hand in his. "We share a common faith," he pointed out. "We share the same core values. We both value family." He saved his strongest argument for last. "We both love the girls."

She nodded, and tears rolled down her cheeks again. "I do love the girls, so much. And I love you, Bran. But—" She let out a slow breath. "I'm just a wet blanket to you. I'm not any of the things to you that Darla was. She was a gourmet cook. I can't even make spaghetti. Look at what happened when you tried to take me skiing. I can't stand sports and crowds and noise. You need someone who will jump out of planes with you. That's not me." Her voice caught. "You need someone like—Sheba."

Brandon was horrified. "Sheba?" he said in disbelief. "Where did that come from? Morgan, just because—"

Her voice shook. "I overheard her at the New Year's Eve party. She's had her eye on you for a long time, and she means to have you."

"Well, she's not going to get me!" Brandon shouted. He

shook his head in frustration. "Morgan, how could you think that I would give a woman like her a second look?"

Morgan closed her eyes, and began to shake. Tears rolled down her cheeks. "Bran, you need—someone—who—" She could hardly get the words out. "Who can—give you a son—the—the brother the girls—want." April and Shelbie had made another mention during dinner about wanting a baby brother, and Bran had shut them down.

Brandon scooted closer to her. "Morgan, we talked about that, and it doesn't matter. *I love you.*" He lowered his voice to an impassioned whisper and said it again.

She blotted her eyes with a tissue and sighed. "I don't doubt your love for me, Bran," she said sadly, "but I wonder if it's really enough. I feel so inadequate most of the time because I'm always saying no to things that you want to do, or getting hurt. You travel in circles that are completely foreign to me. And when we do things that I like to do, you're bored and you fall asleep or you're trying to get service on your cell, or—"

"Morgan, I'm so sorry. Let me—"

Morgan slipped out of his arms and stood. "I need to go."

Brandon stood and put his arms around her. The food from dinner swirled in his stomach, and he felt the first stages of panic. "Morgan, I—" His voice cracked. He swallowed. "I can't lose you, babe, I can't."

Tears ran down her cheeks. "I—I just need some time to think, Bran. Please, just give me some space."

She leaned up and kissed his cheek, and then she was gone.

45

OVER THE NEXT four days, Brandon could hardly function. It was like losing Darla all over again. He couldn't eat, couldn't sleep, and couldn't concentrate on anything. Fortunately, he only had one surgery scheduled, and he was able to assign it to another doctor. He knew enough to not trust himself to be at the head of an operating table in this state.

Even though it almost killed him, he honored Morgan's request for some space, and didn't call or text her. By Wednesday night, he felt like he'd been wandering in the desert for weeks with no water. Morgan fed his soul, and he felt like he was drying up.

After he got the girls to bed, Brandon went to his room and spent a long time trying to compose a text, but couldn't find the right words. Finally, he typed *I miss you. Could I come by your office tomorrow after work for a few minutes?* He stared at it, and hit send.

He jumped up and busied himself getting his things ready for morning so he wouldn't go crazy. She might already be asleep. She could have turned her phone off. He conjured up every excuse he could think of for why she might not answer him.

When his phoned pinged with an incoming text, he leaped across the room to get it. He read the one-word response.

Yes.

Yes! That one solitary word gave him hope. He felt like he'd gotten his life back. Brandon fell back on his bed, his heart thundering. *Thank you, God!* He drew in great gulps of air. He lay there for a few moments and then got up and opened his top dresser drawer. He reached for the black velvet box, and opened it. The solitaire diamond winked at him, and he reached out and touched it. He was planning to propose to Morgan on their upcoming trip to New York, but desperate times called for desperate measures.

Brandon closed the box, walked into the closet, and put it into his jacket pocket. Then he went online to make another purchase. He wanted everything to be perfect for tomorrow night.

46

MORGAN LOOKED AT the e-mail one more time to make sure she wasn't dreaming. She was sure she'd read it a hundred times since it landed in her inbox a half hour ago.

She leaned back in her chair and covered her mouth with her hands so she wouldn't scream or giggle or laugh out loud. Morgan looked at the time. Brandon would be here any minute, and she couldn't wait to share her good news with him.

Morgan had missed him so much since Saturday night. She'd hardly eaten or slept. She knew now that she had completely over-reacted about Sheba, and couldn't imagine her life without him. Of course they were different. She and Patrick had been too much alike. Brandon was—well, he was her perfect complement. Morgan knew he adored her. *I love him so much, God. We'll make it work.*

She heard a noise at the door, and her heart burst with love when she saw him standing there, tall and handsome and holding a bouquet of calla lilies.

By the time he'd closed the door behind him, she was in his arms. "Bran!" Tears rolled down her cheeks.

"Morgan, I love you so much," he said, his voice cracking. And then his soft, warm lips were on hers.

"I love you, Brandon. I'm so sorry," she said over and over. She couldn't get enough of his kisses, and it seemed that he couldn't, either.

Finally, they had to come up for air. He touched his forehead to hers. "This is where it all began," he said. "Right here in your office. You, me, and these." He held up the bouquet.

Morgan thought that was the sweetest thing she had ever heard. She smiled at him. "Where did you find calla lilies in Chicago in January?"

He locked his arms around her. "I didn't. I had to order them online and have them delivered, overnight." He pulled her closer.

This man is so amazing. "Oh, Bran," she sighed. "You make me feel so special."

"You *are* special," he said. "And I have some other special things planned for tonight, starting with dinner at Autumn Evening—but not on the patio."

She smiled. "That sounds perfect. But I have some amazing news to share with you first!" She took his hand and led him to a chair, and before she could sit down in the one next to him, he pulled her onto his lap. Morgan giggled and looped her arms around his neck. She was so happy, she could hardly get the words out. "I got an unexpected e-mail this afternoon. Do you remember what NCAT is?"

He nodded. "The National Consortium for Art Therapy."

"Very good, doctor," she said with a grin. "You're looking at the NCAT Art Therapist of the Year!"

Brandon's eyes lit up. "Morgan, that's fantastic!"

"I can't believe it, Bran. People usually don't get that award until they've been in the field for a really long time. I went back and looked, and I'm by far the youngest recipient. I just can't believe it!"

Morgan wondered if he'd lost as much sleep over the past few days as she had. His gorgeous eyes looked as tired as Morgan's felt, but they sparkled at her now. "I am so, so proud of you, babe," he whispered.

She smoothed one hand over his lapel. "And that's not all." She took a breath. "I was also the recipient of NCAT's annual research grant. I made a proposal for something that I'd like to discuss with you."

"With me?"

She nodded. "I, um—well, I did an informal research study a few years ago about using art therapy with high school athletes who had been injured, and I submitted this proposal hoping to pilot it with professional athletes, and hopefully publish it." She searched his eyes, anxious for his reaction.

"Wow. I've—I've never thought of that," Brandon said. "You know, six months ago I would have thought that was crazy, but you, Dr. Anderson—" he gave her a quick peck on the lips. "You are so amazing, and so smart, and so beautiful, and right now, you could talk me into doing *anything* for you." He wiggled his eyebrows and swooped in for another kiss that was definitely not a quick peck.

Morgan laid her head on his shoulder. "No one has ever received the research grant *and* the award in the same year. I'm the first."

"I'm so proud of you," Brandon said, and kissed her temple.

She straightened up. "Will you be my date for the award ceremony?"

"You bet," he said, grinning at her. "Name the day and time, and I'll be there in my tux."

Morgan almost swooned, thinking of him in a tux. She ran her fingers through his hair. "It's always here in Chicago," she said, "so we don't have to travel. Sunday evening, February first."

A shadow crossed his features. "Morgan, tell me you didn't just say Sunday the first."

"Yes, that's what I said. It's on Sunday the first. Weekend after next."

Brandon closed his eyes. "Morgan, it can't be. That's Super Bowl Sunday."

"What?"

"Sweetheart, it's the *Super Bowl*. And the Bears are playing in the Super Bowl this year. I have to be there. I was going to invite you to come with me."

"I know about the Super Bowl," she said, fiddling with the knot of his tie. Since Morgan had been dating Brandon, she'd been proud of how she'd kept up with Chicago's pro sport teams. "Is the game at Soldier Field? You could go there for a while, and then meet me at the award ceremony. It's at the Chesterfield."

Brandon looked at her somberly. "Babe, the game is in San Diego." His eyes were filled with pain.

Morgan felt her world starting to crumble. *No!* "San Diego?" she croaked.

"Morgan, I'm so sorry."

"You can't get out of it?"

He shook his head. "Even if I could—Morgan, it's the *Super Bowl*."

She crossed her arms. "It's a game, Bran," she said hotly. "I'm getting two very prestigious awards that I've worked very hard for." He didn't say anything. "This is important to me."

He squeezed his eyes shut and opened them again. "And I'm so proud of you, Morgan, but I can't—I can't be there, babe. I'm so sorry." He tightened his hold on her.

Morgan pushed away from him, stood, and walked around to her desk. She couldn't remember when she'd ever been so angry. "A few minutes ago, I was amazing, and smart, and beautiful, and you would do *anything* for me." She stood behind her chair.

Brandon stood. "Morgan," he pleaded, "If it were any other night, I would be there. But I *cannot* get out of this." He rammed a hand through his hair. "I promise, I will make it up to you." He thought about the ring in his pocket and looked at her for a few silent seconds. "Can we just—are you—well, can we go to dinner now?"

Morgan wanted to scream. "I'm not going anywhere with you, Brandon," she said in a low voice. "You need to leave."

"Morgan—"

"Leave now." Her voice was stronger now. His mouth dropped open. "I mean it."

He walked to the door, paused, and looked at her with tortured eyes. "Morgan—I love you."

"You've made your choice. Goodbye, Brandon."

47

WHEN BRANDON PULLED his SUV into the garage, he couldn't even remember driving home from Morgan's office. He was in a complete stupor. Fortunately, the girls had a dance lesson tonight, so they and Sara wouldn't be home for at least another hour. He couldn't face anyone tonight.

Brandon shuffled into the kitchen and just stood there. He was haunted by the memories of Morgan being there with the girls the other night when he came in. All his hopes and dreams of making a life with her had turned to ashes. Brandon didn't know how he was going to fix this. *It's impossible. I can't be in two places at once.*

He got a drink of water and went upstairs, got out of his suit and threw it across a chair, and got into bed. *Not feeling well, going to bed early,* he texted his sister. *Hug and kiss the girls goodnight for me.*

He lay there for hours, numb, but unable to sleep. When his phone pinged with an incoming text, he was shocked to see that it was 10:30. He hadn't heard Sara and the girls come in.

It was Landon. *If my wife knew I was talking with the enemy, I'd be sleeping in the garage tonight. Are you ok?*

Brandon sat up and put his head in his hands. After a few moments, he texted back. *No.*

I'm here if you need me, bro. Now or later.

Brandon heaved a huge sigh. He sat there silently for several minutes. *Who schedules anything on Super Bowl Sunday?* he finally texted.

I'm sorry, Landon texted back.

I can't talk about this now.

It's okay. Praying for you.

Thanks.

Brandon got back under the covers and lay there staring at nothing in the darkness. The next thing he knew, his alarm was going off. He didn't think he'd been asleep for long. He moved like an automaton through his morning routine. When he walked into the kitchen, Sara and the girls were there.

"You feeling better?" Sara asked.

"No, but I have to go into work," he responded quietly.

April and Shelbie seemed to know that something was wrong. They got up and came to him, tugging on his pant legs. Brandon's heart gave a painful squeeze. His girls meant everything to him. They would always be there for him.

He gathered them up in his arms. Soon, they'd be too big for him to lift both of them up at once. He buried his face in their sweet, little-girl-scented hair.

"I love you, Daddy," April said, and gave him a peck on the cheek.

"Why you sad, Daddy?" Shelbie frowned at him.

He tickled them and they began to squeal and laugh. He set them down and kissed both their cheeks. "I'm not sad! Who could ever be sad around the two best girls in the whole world?"

They skipped back to resume their breakfast. Sara eyed Brandon warily. "Are you okay, Brandon?" she said softly.

"I'm fine. I have a boatload of work to do today. I'm headed to San Diego on Monday." He poured coffee into his travel mug and headed for the door. "See you tonight," he said, and walked out the door.

48

MORGAN UNLOCKED HER office door and wrinkled her nose. She'd had patients and field visits the end of last week, and hadn't been back to her office since the night Brandon left. Her eye went immediately to the trash can, where she could see the wilted calla lilies sticking out. She set her things down, grabbed the can, and marched down the hall with it until she found a larger trash receptacle, and dumped everything in.

When she got back to her office, she poured some oil in her diffuser and turned it on. Then she played the messages on her answering machine while she got things out of her bag and got organized.

The first two messages weren't important, but Morgan stopped when she heard the next one. "Morgan, it's Joyce Sheldon. I'm so sorry I've been out of touch since you left your message several weeks ago. My mother died and I've been in Ohio dealing with that and getting my dad settled in a new place." Morgan's heart went out to the woman. "Anyway, I'm back in Chicago now and trying to get caught up, but I should have some time to meet with you later this week if you're still interested in fostering. All the best to you in the new year. Bye."

Morgan sighed and sat down. With the holidays and all the ups and downs with her and Bran, she hadn't thought at all about her hope to become a foster parent. Maybe this was her answer, if she and Bran were over. But right now she didn't have the emotional energy to think about something as important as taking on the responsibility for a child. She had to give herself time to heal first. Maybe she would call Joyce and see what she thought.

The next message began to play, and there was silence. Morgan looked up from what she was doing, and her heart slammed in her chest when Brandon's voice came on. "Morgan, I'm just getting on the plane for San Diego. I love you, babe, more than I ever thought I could love anyone. We'll talk when I get back—"

Just hearing his voice was torture. Morgan didn't want to hear another word. She punched her finger to stop the message replay, and hit *delete.* If only there were a delete button to erase him out of her head and her heart.

Of course he'd called her office phone. She hadn't taken any of his calls since the other night, nor answered any of his texts. It was over. Morgan couldn't take any more of the roller-coaster emotions of this romance, and Brandon had clearly shown where his priorities lay, it didn't matter how many times he told her he loved her, or how amazing his kisses were.

Stop thinking about him.

Her phone pinged with a text, and Morgan just stared at it, afraid to touch it. But she couldn't ignore it. She had students and patients who depended on her.

She took a deep breath and checked it. The text was from Kelsea. *How are you, Morgy? I'm worried about you.*

Morgan sighed and tucked a strand of hair behind her ear. *I'm swamped with work. I'm fine.* She tossed the phone back on her desk and sank into her chair. Tears filled her eyes. Morgan's future stretched before her, bleak and lonely. She would only be able to spend holidays with her sister and her family if none of Landon's family was around.

Of course she had called her sister right after Bran had left her office the other night, and poured the whole story out and cried and cried. Kelsea agreed that it was an impossible situation and that if Bran really loved Morgan, he wouldn't think twice about where to be. That he was even considering going to San Diego was bad enough in Kelsea's mind.

Morgan wondered how things were in the St. Louis St. Clair household.

She opened her computer and began sorting through her e-mails. She straightened her spine and took a deep breath. *You're Dr. Morgan Anderson, NCAT Art Therapist of the Year and recipient of the annual research grant. You are so blessed to have a fulfilling career and friends who respect and care for you, and a mom and a sister who love you.*

Her eye wandered to a hand-drawn picture in a frame on her desk, a Christmas gift from April. Four figures were holding hands. They were labeled, Daddy, Miss Morgy, April, and Shelbie. *My family,* the title read.

Morgan put her head in her hands and burst into tears.

49

BRANDON PULLED HIS hotel room door closed and walked down the hall. Another long night of tossing and turning had passed. He had big, dark circles under his eyes and knew he looked awful. Someone had made a comment about it yesterday and he'd made up a story about being under the weather.

He'd been in San Diego since last Monday, trying to lose himself in the revelry of the most celebrated week in sports. He ran himself ragged from sunup to sundown, missing nothing. Desperately trying to fill the gaping hole in his heart with noise and people.

It wasn't working.

And now it was Sunday morning. Game day. He rode the elevator down and headed for the breakfast buffet, even though the thought of food held no interest for him. Brandon saw a knot of people gathered around someone. The familiar sight of TV cameras and microphones told the story. Something was happening, and the media was there to get it on tape.

It was Kyle Jordanski, one of the Bears' back-up quarterbacks. Brandon had gotten to know him a little bit earlier in the week and thought he was a stand-up guy. They'd made plans to get together when they returned to Chicago. Brandon walked up to the edge of the crowd to listen.

"Well, like I said, they've gotten her stabilized, and the baby is safe for now, but I'm headed home to be with them," Kyle said.

"When did her labor start?" a reporter asked.

"Sandi called me last night around ten, and her dad came to stay with our daughter while Sandi's mom went to the hospital with her. They admitted her and are trying to stop the labor." He smiled. "They want my son to cook for another two weeks at least." A titter went around the group.

Another reporter pushed a microphone closer. "Kyle, how does it feel to be giving up a chance to play in the Super Bowl? Hasn't that been your dream since you were a boy? And the Bears have been waiting for this day for years."

"Was it a hard choice to make?" someone else called out.

"Well, of course I've been looking forward to it, too, but this is my wife, my son, my family. The choice was easy," he said. "I made the choice the day that I took vows for better or for worse. Even before that, really, when I chose to love Sandi. Other than my salvation, she's the most precious gift that God has given me, her and our children."

Jordanski flashed his trademark smile that the fans loved, and Brandon heard the cameras clicking all around him, recording the moment for history. "This is a game," Kyle continued. "My life is waiting for me back in Chicago." He waved. "I appreciate your prayers for Sandi and the baby. Thanks, guys."

The reporters shouted more questions, and Kyle moved away with his agent, Tom Kirby. Other Bears security personnel formed a phalanx around the two men and they began to walk away. Suddenly, Brandon had the strongest urge to talk to Kyle.

"Kyle!" He shouted. Jordanski turned and his eyes lit up with recognition. Brandon caught up to him.

"Hey, Brandon," Kyle said as the security detail took a step back. He extended his hand for a shake.

"I'm sorry to hear about your wife and baby. They're in my prayers."

"Thanks, I appreciate that. I really do want to get together when things settle down."

"Kyle, they're holding the plane for us," Tom Kirby said. "We need to go."

Jordanski nodded at Brandon. "Take care, doc."

"Thanks, Kyle. You, too." Brandon stood rooted to the spot, watching the cluster of men as they moved down the hallway, getting smaller and smaller until they turned the corner and disappeared.

Jordanski's words echoed in Brandon's head. *This is a game.* The same exact words that Morgan had used. *My life is waiting for me back in Chicago.*

Brandon's life flashed before his eyes. He hung his head. *And I'm 2,000 miles away.*

50

MORGAN SHOULD BE enjoying herself. She was surrounded by people she'd known for years, ever since she began college. The art therapy community was like family to her. She'd seen people tonight that she hadn't seen in a very long time, and it felt like they'd never been apart. Everyone was heaping love and praise on her. They respected her as a person and as an artist and art therapist, and it should have filled her with indescribable joy. This should have been one of the happiest nights of her life.

Instead, she felt dead, empty, and hopeless. If a million people had been here to celebrate this night with her, it wouldn't have mattered without the one person who mattered most to her in the world.

Morgan still couldn't think of him without her stomach going into painful spasms. She looked down at her plate. She'd eaten hardly anything even though the food at the Chesterfield was some of the best in all of Chicago.

She had invited her mother to the awards banquet, but Beth had come down with the flu yesterday. Morgan felt horribly guilty that her first response when her mother called was relief. Beth knew that her daughter and Brandon weren't seeing one another anymore, but they hadn't talked about it much, and Morgan didn't think she could take an evening of her mom's tender pity.

Her mother would also notice that Morgan's clothes were hanging on her. When she had put on her favorite go-to "little black dress" tonight, she'd had to put several pins in it.

"Morgan?" She felt a hand squeeze her shoulder. It was her colleague, Juanita Ross. "You're a million miles away."

"Sorry, Juanita." Morgan tried to dredge up a smile.

Juanita squeezed her hand. "Are you okay?"

"I'm fine."

"They want to begin in a few minutes. Do you want to visit the powder room first?"

Morgan stood and collected her purse. "Um, yeah, sure." When she returned to the meeting room, people were milling around visiting, and Juanita waved at her from the stage. Morgan joined her and Dr. Ed Faraday, the current president of NCAT. Ed indicated where Morgan should sit, and she took her seat next to Juanita. Two other NCAT board members were seated on the stage as well.

Dr. Faraday stepped to the podium and quieted the crowd. He gave the usual greeting, the acknowledgement of the fine meal provided by the catering staff at the Chesterfield, and then launched into his speech. Morgan pasted a smile on her face and nodded in all the right places. She rose when they presented her with the award and then the plaque for the research grant, and accepted congratulations from her colleagues on stage. She smiled for the photographer and stepped to the podium, and concentrated on forming cohesive sentences to express her deep appreciation to everyone there.

And then she sank back into her seat to thunderous applause, and wished that she could just go home and cry her heart out. Morgan knew that people expected her to stay around and socialize, but she knew a back exit, and planned to escape the minute this was over.

Morgan didn't think anything of it when a stagehand hurried to Dr. Faraday and pressed a note into his hand. He opened it and read it. "Folks, if you would take your seats, please" he said to the crowd, "someone else has asked to say a few words tonight in Dr. Anderson's honor."

Morgan couldn't imagine who it could be. And then, she looked past Dr. Faraday and she saw him.

Bran.

51

BRANDON TOOK A deep breath, straightened his lapels, and walked out onto the stage. He saw Morgan's look of utter shock, and hoped she wouldn't faint. He wanted more than anything to gather her into his arms and never let go, but he had to fix things first.

Brandon stepped to the podium. "Um, hi. I'm Dr.—" he swallowed, and it occurred to him that he didn't want to use his title here and be mistaken for the wrong kind of doctor. *How ironic.* "I'm Brandon," he corrected himself. "Brandon St. Clair." He scanned the crowd. About a third of the attendees were men. "I'm just curious—could I ask—has anyone heard the score of the game?" His phone had died in the cab on the way in from the airport.

Nervous male laughter rippled through the room. "Ten-seven, Bears at the half," a man called out.

"JoJo caught a pass with eight seconds left and ran it in for the TD," another man shouted. There were a few claps and whistles. Brandon smiled to himself. JoJo Collins' knee had healed beautifully.

Brandon nodded. "Are any of you men here instead of at a Super Bowl Party, to be with the woman you love?"

He saw nods and smiles, heard some more claps and whistles.

"Well, that's why I'm here, too," Brandon said. He turned around and looked at Morgan, his beautiful Morgan. He turned back to the audience. "I—well, I've been in San Diego this week. Because of my work, I've had the privilege of traveling with the Bears and experiencing Super Bowl week out there."

Brandon could tell that he had the audience's rapt attention, especially that of the men. He rubbed his chin. "So, I had a reserved seat in one of the boxes at the stadium, but I was miserable. I'm in love with Dr. Morgan Anderson, and I knew I needed to be here, so I left San Diego and flew home in time to see her receive these fantastic awards."

After Kyle Jordanski left, Brandon had run after him and begged him to hold the plane while he dashed upstairs to his room and packed his things.

He turned and looked at Morgan, who was fighting tears. "I am so proud of you, babe."

Brandon felt his face heat up as the room exploded with applause and whistles. As it faded away, a booming male voice called out, "Man, you must *really* love her!" The crowd laughed.

Brandon nodded. "Yes, I do," he said confidently. "I love her more than anything in this entire world." He turned and looked at Morgan again, and tears were streaming down her cheeks. He held out his hand and she rose gracefully and came to him.

He stepped away from the podium and took both her

hands. "I resigned my position," he said softly. He'd taken care of that with one phone call from the plane to the Center's board chairman.

Her teary eyes went wide. "You resigned your position?"

"Is there an echo in here?" Brandon resisted the urge to laugh but instead, squeezed her hands, and she squeezed back. "Yes, and it was the right decision." He smiled at her sheepishly. "You're now dating an unemployed doctor." He swallowed. "If you'll have me back."

"Hey!" the man with the booming voice called out. "Somebody turn the overhead mikes on. We want to hear this!"

The crowd burst into laughter and applause, and Brandon grinned at Morgan and let out a breath.

"Anything you want to say to me, you say to them." She dipped her chin at the audience. "These are my friends."

"Fair enough," Brandon said with a nod. It didn't matter to him. If there were a million people in the room, it wouldn't matter. He had eyes only for Morgan.

Brandon waited for the audience to quiet down. He knew he had one chance to get this right. He gazed into her beautiful emerald eyes. "You know mine and my brother's mantra is *go big or go home,*" he said boldly. He heard his voice coming across the PA system, and it gave him strength. "That's what my life came down to today. I could either *go big*—keep the high-powered job, hang out with professional athletes, fly all over the country and go to the World Series and the Super Bowl." He paused. "Or I could *go home*. I couldn't have it both ways."

"I came home, Morgan. Home to you."

Brandon stepped a little closer to her. "When I lost—my

wife, for days and weeks and months, it felt like my heart wasn't even beating." He took her lovely, graceful hand, the one that created such inspired, beautiful works of art, and placed it over his thundering heart. "Do you feel that, Morgan? That's because of you."

He heard a collective gasp and a swell of murmurs from the crowd as April and Shelbie walked out on stage, holding hands and wearing their red and white Christmas dresses. They looked like two little fair-haired angels. From the wings, Sara gave Brandon a teary smile and a thumbs-up. He'd called her from the plane, and she'd followed his instructions to the letter. A wave of love washed over Brandon for his sister.

Morgan was crying now, and covered her mouth with both hands.

Brandon rubbed her arms. "I brought reinforcements," he said with a smile. The audience laughed.

He felt a tug on his sleeve. "You hafta get down on your knees, Daddy!" Shelbie ordered.

The crowd roared, and Brandon grinned. "I was just getting to that part." He pulled the black velvet box out of his pocket, opened it, and dropped to one knee. "Dr. Morgan Ashley Anderson, I will always come home to you. You keep my heart beating, you complete our family circle. I love you so much, Morgan, and I will love you forever." He looked at the girls, and hoped Sara had coached them well.

"Will you please be our mommy?" April and Shelbie said in unison.

"And will you be my wife?"

52

MORGAN KNEW SHE would never answer two more important questions in her life. Her heart blossomed with love for this family that God had brought to her. But which question to answer first?

She knew what God expected. Her heart would always belong to her husband above all else.

Morgan could hardly speak for the emotion that clogged her throat, so she nodded vigorously. "Yes, Bran, yes," was all she managed to choke out. She saw him slip a ring on her finger, but she didn't even look at it. She reached for him and his strong arms came around her.

Morgan felt a sense of peace wash over her, and never wanted to let him go. But then she felt tapping on her hip, and looked down. There was Shelbie, smiling up at her, and sweet April. She bent down and gathered them in her arms. *My girls.* They were everything she had prayed for. Morgan would never need another child—biological or adopted—to be fulfilled as a mother.

"Of course I'll be your mommy, April and Shelbie. I love you so much."

She picked up Shelbie, and Bran picked up April, and they formed a little circle. Bran leaned over and touched his lips to hers. *All my dreams are coming true.*

Morgan could hardly believe it when the audience cheered. She'd forgotten they were even there. As she looked out over her friends and colleagues, they rose to their feet.

Bran took her hand, and they faced the crowd. The girls were smiling and waving at all the people. After a couple of moments, the noise died down.

"Daddy, and Miss Mommy," Shelbie said in loud, clear voice that echoed through the loud speakers, "are we going to get a baby brother now?"

EPILOGUE

BRANDON MADE ONE last check in the mirror and walked over to the large window overlooking the backyard. In less than hour, he would marry Morgan at the five-acre country property that they had bought together, surrounded by their families and a few close friends. He and the girls had moved in, after selling their too-large and too-pretentious suburban home. The movers brought Morgan's things two days ago, and she was looking forward to setting up housekeeping.

It was the perfect place for them—a rambling, custom-made cedar and stone home overlooking a beautiful pond. Best of all, it was secluded but only ten minutes away from shopping and restaurants, and close to the depot where they could catch the train into Chicago. Brandon was beginning to appreciate the serenity of country life. It would be a great place for their daughters to grow up. As long as Morgan was by his side, he would be happy anywhere.

They were finding ways to compromise. Cross-country skiing was one of them. And last weekend, they'd gone boating on Lake Michigan with some friends and really enjoyed that.

Brandon wanted to start saving for a speedboat. Morgan dreamed of a pontoon boat.

After resigning as Medical Director at the center, Brandon wasn't unemployed for long. They hired him back to build and oversee something that was part of his long-range plan, a sports medicine and orthopedic center for high school and college athletes. He got to name his terms: days only with the occasional emergency surgery and very little travel. The most important thing to Brandon was being available to his wife and family.

He was so proud of Morgan, and knew that she could do anything she set her mind to. He listened patiently as she agonized over how she would juggle her career with her important new roles as wife and mother. After a lot of discussion with him, and prayer, Morgan decided to resign from her art therapy practice, at least until April and Shelbie were in school. The other two therapists in the group were very understanding and gave her an open invitation to come back anytime in the future. Then she had a heartfelt talk with Juanita Ross and they worked out a perfect teaching schedule where Morgan would only have to go into campus two days a week.

There was a fabulous glass-enclosed four-season room on the south side of their home with its own entrance, and she planned to turn that into a studio and do art lessons there, and continue her research. Morgan wanted to get used to being a mom, and then they would pray about becoming foster parents or adopting to grow their family, and let God lead. Both Brandon and Morgan were passionately committed to the idea.

He looked around the master bedroom at the brand-new furniture he and his bride had chosen together, and Morgan's beautiful artwork and other handcrafted accessories that graced the room. Tonight, it would become their oasis. His parents and Grandma Beth were taking the girls with Landon and Kelsea and their family to a nearby hotel with a water park for two nights, and then he and Morgan would pick up April and Shelbie on Wednesday and drive to Indianapolis for a three-day family vacation. The big draw there was the famed children's museum. Then they planned to drive north to Wisconsin where the girls would stay with Brandon's parents, and he and Morgan would enjoy a few more days alone before coming back home to begin their new life as a family.

Brandon's heart was full to overflowing. He closed his eyes and whispered, "You would like her, Dar. She'll be a wonderful mother to your girls." He was amazed at how Morgan thought of little ways to keep Darla's memory alive. She was confident in Brandon's love now, and her tender nurturing had helped April blossom into her sweet, content former self. Brandon couldn't believe it when he recently overheard April talking to one of her little friends. "I had a first mommy who I'll see again in heaven someday, and now I have a second mommy, and I love her very, very much."

Brandon breathed a prayer to God, full of gratitude and thankfulness.

The door opened behind him, and his brother walked in, holding his cell phone. He was dressed in a black tux identical to Brandon's, and his face was serious.

Landon closed the door. "Bro, you need to sit down," he said. "We need to talk."

Morgan thought her heart was going to burst with joy. *Today is my first Mother's Day, and my wedding day.* April and Shelbie had woken her up this morning, dropping the "Miss" and calling her *Mommy* for the very first time. They covered her with hugs and kisses and gave her homemade cards. She loved them so much.

Brandon had stood in the doorway with a cup of coffee, smiling and watching her with the girls. As Morgan stared at him, she knew exactly what he was thinking. Tomorrow and all the mornings thereafter for the rest of their lives, she would wake up next to him.

Now, she and her sister were waiting for the ceremony to begin. She stared at the glittering diamond on her left hand. In just a few moments, a beautiful wedding band would rest next to it. "You look stunning, Morgy," Kelsea said. "Your dress is simply amazing."

Morgan loved her wedding dress. It was classic, a simple but elegant creation of satin, lace, and pearls with a vintage flair. When she first saw it—even before she tried it on—she knew she would wear this dress when she married Brandon.

Kelsea dabbed at her eyes. "I hope this waterproof mascara is the real deal, because I know I'm going to cry buckets and I'll look like a raccoon."

"Me, too," Morgan said with a smile. "At least you have an excuse." Kelsea was almost three months pregnant with another set of twins, and could cry at the drop of a hat. Morgan sighed. "But I'm so happy, I know I'll cry nonstop."

There was a knock at the door, and Landon called out. "Can I come in?"

"Yes," Kelsea called back.

He stepped in and stopped. "Hi. Ah, Morgan—I know you didn't want Brandon to see you before the wedding, but we need to come in. It's important."

Morgan's stomach gave a lurch. "Is something wrong?"

To her immense relief, Landon smiled. "No, something is very, very right." He held out his hand to Kelsea. "Come out here with me, sweetheart, and we'll give them a moment." Kelsea and Landon left, and Brandon walked in.

My TDH for life, she thought as her heart fluttered. She never got tired of seeing Bran in a tux. Today, he looked especially rugged and handsome. He closed the door and turned to look at her. His gaze swept from the tips of her toes to the top of her head, where her mother had fashioned an elegant French twist, topped off by flower-covered comb and a flowing veil.

He took a step forward. "Oh, babe," he said, and she could see that his eyes were moist. "You are so, so gorgeous."

In the next moment, she was in his arms, and she whispered between kisses, "so are you. I love you so much, Bran."

"I love you, Morgan." He held her close for another moment, then stepped back. Without breaking eye contact with her, he called out, "you can come in now."

Landon and Kelsea came back into the room, and the four of them stood in a little circle. Landon let out a breath. "Okay. Here's what's happening. A little while ago, I got a phone call from a guy that I went to law school with. We've kept in touch, but I haven't talked with him in a couple of years. He specializes in private adoptions. A fifteen-year-old girl gave birth yesterday, and changed her mind about keeping the baby. Her parents support that decision. She's signed away her rights, and so has the baby's father. It will be a closed adoption.

"Ben—my friend—said that he hadn't thought about me in a long time, but suddenly this morning, after all this happened, he felt a strong urge to call me." Landon looked at Brandon and Morgan. "The baby is full-term and healthy. He's yours if you want him."

"Him?" Morgan croaked. She felt her legs start to buckle, and Brandon's arm came around her waist to steady her.

Landon nodded. "You can pick him up on Wednesday—" Morgan was stunned to see her brother-in-law's eyes well up as he struggled for composure. "In Indianapolis."

Morgan gasped, and her hands flew to her mouth. The room went still, and she heard her heart pounding in her ears. She looked up at Brandon, and tears ran down his cheeks. "Oh, Bran!" she cried, and threw her arms around him. He buried his face in her neck and they both cried.

"This is—the answer—to the girls' prayers," she stammered. She touched his damp cheeks. "We're doing this, right?"

He looked at her somberly. "Only if you're okay with it, if you're ready for it."

There was no doubt in Morgan's mind. *God has given me more than I could ask or think.* "Oh my goodness, yes!" she exclaimed, and Brandon put his arms around her and kissed her. She accepted a handful of tissues from Kelsea, who was crying tears of joy. Morgan looked at Landon. "Doesn't it cost a lot for a private adoption?"

She saw the two brothers exchange a look. "It's taken care of, Morgan," he said quietly, and his eyes shone. "Happy wedding."

"I can't believe this. I can't believe it, thank you, Landon," she said, and gave him a heartfelt hug. Then she fell into her sister's arms. "I'm having a baby on Wednesday!" she squealed.

"Oh, Morgy! Look at how God has answered all of your prayers!" Kelsea wept. The sisters clung to one another, rocking back and forth.

Landon smiled. "If you two can stop crying, I think we need to get this wedding underway. Everyone is here, if you're ready."

Morgan blotted her eyes and looked between the two men. "Did Reagan make it?" They had mailed their older sister an invitation, but didn't receive a response. Phone calls and texts had gone unanswered.

Landon and Brandon exchanged a glance, and Brandon shook his head. "I didn't really expect her to come, but I was hoping she would."

Landon reached for the doorknob.

"Oh, hold on!" Kelsea waved her hands and looked at Brandon and then to Morgan. "I have a card for you from Rose and Ike. Rosie asked me to give it to you just before the ceremony." She rifled through her bag and drew out an envelope, and handed it to Morgan.

Brandon came over to her and they opened it and held the card together. "You read it," she said. Morgan didn't think her voice would hold up.

Brandon's voice was clear and strong. *"Congratulations on your marriage, Morgan and Brandon! I knew last Mother's Day weekend that you were meant to be together. Isn't the Lord wonderful? He has answered your prayers beyond all that you could ask or think! We hope you will never doubt His faithfulness ever again. Give your beautiful daughters a hug from us, and tell them to—"* Brandon's eyes grew wide, and his voice wavered. *"Tell them to take good care of their little brother! Come to St. Jardin on us sometime! We are turning our honeymoon resort into a family resort! Much love, Rosie and Ike."*

Morgan's mouth fell open, as did the others, and all four of them stared at one another for a long moment.

Brandon turned the envelope over. "It's—it's postmarked a week ago," he said in disbelief.

Morgan couldn't believe it. "How—how did she—?" A chill raced down her spine. She and Bran stared at one another.

He held up his hand. "There's more. *"P.S. Did you ever meet the lawyer who contacted you about coming to Chicago, Brandon? That's Ike's oldest nephew, David. He's such a nice young man."*

Brandon's jaw dropped. "David Goldman—he's the one who first called me about the job." He shook his head and looked at Morgan, then to his brother and Kelsea. "Do you mean to tell me that little lady with the pink Converse and pink hair—?" his words dropped off.

Kelsea laughed uproariously. "That Rosie! I do believe she's God's angel, doing His work on this earth!" She and Landon wrapped their arms around one another, and Morgan felt Brandon's arms come around her.

He kissed her forehead and whispered in her ear. "Are you ready to marry me, Miss Morgy? I mean, Dr. Anderson?" His amber eyes danced. "Mrs. St. Clair? Dr. Mrs. St. Clair? Dr. Anderson-St. Clair?" She'd told Bran that she wanted to take his name, but he'd left the decision completely up to her about what to be called professionally, and she was still thinking about it.

Morgan couldn't wait to be his wife and the mother of his daughters and his son. She pulled him close and whispered in his ear. "You can just call me babe."

ABOUT THE AUTHOR

Writing is like breathing to Erin. Stories are running through her mind during most of her waking hours, and by the time she sits down at the computer, the words flow and time ceases to exist.

Erin was raised in Illinois and has lived in many places in the U.S., including on both coasts, but is a Midwest girl at heart. She spent many years as an educator from pre-school through college levels, and currently works in training and internal communications for a major global corporation.

When she's not writing, Erin loves spending time with her children and grandchildren, and playing in the garden (which equates to mostly pulling weeds) at her central Iowa home. Her secret indulgence is plain M&Ms.

Connect with Erin!
Email: ESQwrites@gmail.com
Website: www.ESQwrites.com
Facebook: ESQwrites
Twitter: @ESQwrites

COMING SOON

Book Three in the
St. Clair Family Series

BAIT AND SWITCH

Reagan St. Clair is on the run. Her reporter's nose for news has landed her too close to something sinister, and she's not safe.

Sara St. Clair is the "caboose" of the family, born when her three siblings were in their teens. She's always been *Peanut* to them, but she's an adult now, and wishes they would take her seriously. Sara is at a crossroads in life with no idea of what to do. More than anything, she wants to make a difference in someone's life.

Dane Corsica is a young, successful DEA agent who's charged himself with keeping Reagan safe. They need a place to hide, and end up on the island of St. Jardin at a honeymoon resort, but the pretense of posing as a newlywed couple is difficult for both of them. A long-ago betrayal has caused Reagan to trust no one, and Dane has his own reasons for guarding his heart.

When Sara arrives at the resort, things get even more mixed up. Dane finds himself attracted to not just one, but both St. Clair sisters. When Sara is mistaken for Reagan and kidnapped, Dane has to choose which one to protect.

And Rosie, the pink-haired matchmaker, has to figure out who belongs with whom.

The third and final installment in the *St. Clair Family Series* will entertain you and keep you on the edge of your seat until the final page.

See the next page for a sneak peek of the first three chapters of *Bait and Switch,* Book Three in the St. Clair Family Series. Available January 1, 2019 in print and eBook.

BAIT AND SWITCH

REAGAN

REAGAN ST. CLAIR slipped into a chair on the back row and adjusted her designer sunglasses on the bridge of her nose. Good. No one noticed her late arrival.

She smoothed the full skirt of her flowered halter sundress over her knees. The dress, high wedge sandals, and the luxurious blond curls flowing from under her oversized couture summer hat were so far from her usual look that surely, no one would recognize her.

Reagan's right leg began to tremble. She clasped her hands tightly together and pressed them against her knee, willing the shaking to stop.

I hate weddings.

The image of Paul in bed with her best friend still had the power to sear Reagan's memory, even ten years later. His and Reagan's wedding was just a month away, and everything had to be canceled, despite his pleading and begging for exoneration.

Reagan could forgive, but not for infidelity.

Her gaze drifted over the small bridal party gathered in front of a rose-covered arch and rested on her brother Landon, standing as best man for their younger brother, Brandon. The St. Clair men cut fine figures in their tuxedos. Standing at six foot four, they could pass for twins even though they were almost a year apart in age. Their features were nearly identical, the only difference being that Landon was blond and Brandon's hair was dark brown.

There looked to be less than a hundred people gathered for the small, intimate Sunday afternoon wedding. From the back, Reagan recognized a few older relatives that she hadn't seen in years. She supposed the others in attendance were from the bride's family, or some of her and Brandon's colleagues.

"Join hands, please," the minister said. Brandon turned to face his bride, Morgan, and the look of pure love and joy on her brother's face nearly broke through Reagan's façade. If anyone deserved happiness, it was Brandon. His first wife of over a decade, Darla, had been tragically killed in an automobile accident two years ago. Reagan hadn't met Brandon's bride yet, and hoped she didn't have to today.

Two little blond girls in pink and lavender flowered dresses stood with them. They had to be Brandon's daughters, April and Shelbie. Reagan had seen them only once, at their mother's funeral. She recalled the maelstrom of emotions she felt when meeting them for the first time: incredible sadness for their loss, an unexpected overwhelming connection with them upon the realization that they were her flesh and blood, and a complete lack of knowledge of how to interact with such small children.

The early afternoon sun beat down on the garden wedding, and Reagan was happy for her ridiculous hat. She craned her neck to get a better view. Morgan was similar in coloring to Darla, but tall and slender. Morgan and Brandon had met exactly a year ago on Mother's Day at a family event, yet another one Reagan had missed.

She would have missed this family event, too, if she didn't need a place to hide. After this current mess with her job was over, Reagan was going to do some serious soul searching and figure out how to reconnect with her family.

Her leg began to tremble again, and before she could reach for it, a man slipped into the seat next to her. He wrapped his hand around hers and squeezed.

Dane. Her comrade-in-arms, her best friend. Always there for her. Reagan let out a breath and squeezed back.

"Breathe, Reagan," he whispered in her ear. "We'll get through this."

2

DANE

DANE CORSICA SLIPPED a casual arm around Reagan's bare, tanned shoulder and took the opportunity to glance behind them. He did a sweep one way and then the other. An outdoor wedding was a logistical nightmare from a security vantage point. Too many ways in and out. But Dane was convinced they hadn't been followed.

He smiled to himself as one of Reagan's blond curls brushed against his fingers. Who knew she could be so gorgeous? Dane had known her for four years and had never seen her in a dress, or any makeup save a dash of lip gloss. The absence of Reagan St. Clair's signature long, dark brunette braid was the most dramatic change of all.

It was a good disguise, one that might save her life.

Dane resisted the urge to yawn. They'd been on the run for almost seventy-two hours, and needed to get completely underground. Dane didn't know who he could trust.

But Reagan did.

When she'd pitched her idea for them to come to the Chicago area for this family wedding, Dane was completely against it. Despite that Reagan was distant from her family, she insisted that she still wanted to be part of this day and see her brother get married. And since they had to get out of Florida and go *somewhere*, why not go to Illinois?

He'd finally relented, and told her it would work for the short term. But then, he would have to find a better solution, a deep, off-grid place to keep both of them safe while he unraveled this mess. The problem was, he couldn't go to any of his usual sources. Reagan insisted that her brother, Landon, could find something for them.

Dane had never seen Reagan so certain, so resolute, and he was out of options. So here they were, mere feet away from someone Dane had never met, but whom he would have to trust to keep both himself and Reagan alive and safe.

It went against everything the DEA had taught Dane, but he trusted Reagan, and Reagan trusted her brother. That would have to be good enough for now.

"I now pronounce you man and wife," the minister announced. He smiled at the groom. "Brandon, you may kiss your bride." Dane came out of agent mode just long enough to witness the bridal couple's loving embrace. He looked away.

"Ladies and gentlemen, I'm proud to introduce, for the first time, Dr. Brandon and Dr. Morgan St. Clair!" *That's right, Reagan said he's an MD and she has a PhD.* The audience broke into applause.

Dane tightened his arm around Reagan. "You ready?" He felt her nod. "It's up to you now."

3

REAGAN

REAGAN KNEW SHE would have just a split second to catch Landon's attention. *Please, God, let him remember.* Then she winced inwardly. It was highly unlikely that the Almighty would listen to her. They hadn't been on good terms in years.

Reagan had placed herself on the aisle so that she would have the best chance of making eye contact with her brother. She watched her nieces skip by, hand-in-hand. Then came their father and new mother, their faces bursting with joy. Brandon didn't even look her way. If Reagan had been holding up a flashing neon sign announcing her presence, she doubted he would have noticed.

Here we go. Next came Landon with the matron of honor, his dark-haired wife, Kelsea, who was also Morgan's sister. That's how Brandon and Morgan had met. Reagan lifted a hand to touch the brim of her hat, and the movement caught her brother's eye.

The instant his eyes connected with hers, Reagan moved her hand an inch and tugged on her right earlobe.

Score. Landon's amber eyes widened for a split second, but he didn't break stride, and he and Kelsea were gone.

Reagan casually turned to Dane. "He saw me," she murmured.

"Good job," he whispered. He looked around. "Let's get out of here before any of the other guests start coming by." That was fine with Reagan. She didn't want to chance seeing her parents or her sister. Not until this case was closed and she was safe again.

They rose, and Dane took her hand, pulling her behind a row of tall bushes. "There's an unlocked shed about fifty yards to the south," he said. "Down a slight slope and around behind some trees. You're sure your brother will know to follow us there?"

Reagan nodded. "Positive. He'll be watching me. Our old signal meant *trouble, meet me right away.*" It was from long ago when she and her brothers had fancied themselves amateur detectives in their Wisconsin hometown, but Dane didn't need to know that.

"Well, if anyone else notices us slipping away, they'll just think I want to be alone with the most beautiful woman here." Dane winked at her.

"In your dreams, Corsica," Reagan smirked. In all the years that she and Dane had worked together, he'd never crossed the line, probably because Reagan had never given him any encouragement. He was handsome, to be sure, and the best agent—DEA, FBI, or otherwise—that Reagan had ever worked with. But he was also nine years younger than her (he thought it was only seven since Reagan had fudged about her age), and that was too much. It just didn't feel right to her. Sometimes when she made a pop culture reference from her era, Dane would look at her blankly.

Despite that, he was incredibly mature for his age, and one of the best friends Reagan had ever had. But sometimes, when you tried to make it something more, the friendship didn't survive. And Reagan needed all the friends she could get.

The reception was set up on the deck behind Brandon and Morgan's cedar home on a rolling country property west of Chicago. It was a beautiful setting. From their vantage point behind the bushes, Reagan watched the crowd making its way up to the deck. She thought she recognized a couple of her cousins. Then her heart gave a lurch as she saw her parents, each holding the hand of a small girl and boy. Those must be Landon and Kelsea's twins. She swallowed. *More next-generation St. Clairs.* She felt a familiar twinge of regret that she would probably never give her parents grandchildren. Then followed the ever-present justification that given her time-consuming career and discomfort around children, it was probably for the best.

"Dear heaven, who is *that?*" Dane hissed into her ear. Reagan followed his eye to a petite young woman in a flowered sundress, with thick, honey-blond hair that cascaded halfway down her back. She had sparkling brown eyes, dimples, and a thousand-watt smile. As she greeted someone, her melodious laugh floated to them on the breeze.

"That's my sister, Sara." Sara looked even more grown-up than she had just a few months ago at Christmas.

"She's a little taller than you, but other than that, she could be your twin," Dane murmured. His eyes were riveted on Sara. "Your *much* younger twin," he added.

Reagan bumped her shoulder against his arm. "Gee, thanks," she drawled. But he was right. It hadn't occurred to her, but she and Sara looked very much alike except for their hair color. Now that Reagan was disguised as a blonde, the resemblance was a bit eerie. "She's, um, fifteen years younger than me."

Dane frowned at her. "Really?" *Oops. He's probably trying to do the math.*

Reagan nodded. "She was mom and dad's surprise. The boys were twelve and thirteen when Sara was born. They've always called her *Peanut.*"

Dane and Reagan began to stroll toward a line of trees, and the ground got a little more uneven. Dane put his hand around Reagan's waist to steady her. "I don't want you to fall off those shoes," he said drily.

Reagan resisted the urge to laugh. "Thanks. These sure aren't my Birkenstocks," she retorted. She picked her way gingerly around a tree root.

She saw the wooden shed in the distance, and in another twenty seconds or so, they reached it. Dane pulled the door open and ushered her in, then pulled the door almost closed, leaving a sliver of an opening.

Reagan's eyes adjusted to the dark, and she took off her sunglasses and her hat, and set them on a short stack of wooden crates. Dust motes danced in the sunlight streaming in from a west-facing window. The shed contained a riding lawn mower, wheelbarrow, and the usual yard implements. "This isn't so bad."

"Well, I should be able to scope out a good hiding place," Dane said with a smile. He didn't say anything, and seemed to be perusing her. "I don't think I've ever seen you in a dress."

Reagan let out a breath and fingered her skirt. "Yeah, it's been a while." She thought for a moment. "Maybe the South Florida Press Awards Banquet, three years ago?"

"Yeah, I wasn't there," Dane said with a laugh. "You look completely different without your braid."

"Don't I know it?" Reagan said. Without it, she felt like she was missing a friend.

There was a soft tap at the door, and Dane sprang in front of her, his hand moving quickly inside his jacket. He turned his head and put a finger to his lips.

"Reagan?" came the whisper through the crack in the door. Dane nodded.

"Yes, come in," she said softly. Dane took a step to the side. The door opened, and Landon entered. He reached for Reagan, and she saw Dane pull the door closed behind him.

"Oh my gosh, Reagan." Landon's arms came around her, strong and secure. Reagan felt rare tears coming to her eyes. "What are you doing here? You haven't been answering any of our texts or calls, so I figured you were chasing a story." He pulled back and looked at her. "What's with the hair?" He fingered a curl and smiled. "You look like Peanut."

"I know," Reagan replied. She couldn't go soft now. Dane materialized at her side, and Reagan cleared her throat. "Landon, this is Dane Corsica." The two men shook hands. "Dane's DEA."

Landon didn't blink. He looked at Dane. "You armed?"

Dane pulled one side of his jacket back to reveal his holster.

Landon nodded, and looked back to Reagan. "What's going on?"

Reagan exchanged a glance with Dane. She pulled a

dollar bill out of her purse and held it out to her brother. "I want to hire you as my attorney."

Landon tilted his head at her. He pocketed the bill and looked between her and Dane, his features serious. "Okay, anything you tell me is now protected by attorney-client privilege."

Reagan let out a breath. "Well, the short story is that I work with the DEA sometimes on news stories, and Dane and I trade favors." Landon's eyes darkened a shade.

"Not those kind of favors," Dane muttered. Reagan's face burned.

"Reporters and agents have mutually beneficial relationships," she explained.

Landon rolled his eyes. "Yeah, that sounds a lot better, sis. Go on," he prodded.

Reagan was aware of Dane standing next to her. Why was she flustered? "So anyway, Dane has been working a case undercover, and I got an anonymous tip and went in undercover to investigate on my own, and we ended up at a meeting together, in Miami. It's a drug case connected to Cuba."

Landon frowned. "Sounds like just another day in South Florida." Dane smirked.

"Right," Reagan said. "So anyway, Dane and I ended up at this meeting, and neither of us knew the other one was going to be there. We left separately, and arranged to meet up at one of our normal drop spots where we leave information for each other. But one of us was followed, and we were shot at."

"What?" Landon asked sharply. "Were you hit?"

Dane shook his head. "We managed to get away, but we

don't know which one of us was followed, or by whom. Reagan—"

Landon put his hand up. "Hold it." He turned his palm up.

"Oh, got it," Dane said, and produced a dollar bill. Landon slid it in his pocket. "Go on."

Dane nodded. "When we began sharing information, we started making headway. This story has the potential to be really big. I snuck home and got a few things that I needed to go underground, and planned to finish making the arrangements the next day. But Friday morning, it was all over the news in Miami that the two of us were being sought for questioning about this drug case. I think somebody turned on us."

Reagan picked up the thread. "We needed to get out of Florida, and I really wanted to come to Brandon's wedding, so I convinced Dane to come here."

Dane put his hands on his hips. "I have a private network that I use in situations like this, to find safe houses or get cash or weapons to me, but obviously I can't trust anyone." He paused. "I'm not willing to chance it. So we're completely on our own."

Landon palmed the back of his neck and looked at his sister. He let out a breath. "You always had to be Nancy Drew," he muttered. A smile tugged at the corner of his lips.

Reagan rolled her eyes and tried not to laugh. "He and Brandon were the Hardy Boys," she said to Dane, "but they grew up to be a lawyer and a doctor instead."

Landon looked at his sister with pride. "And you grew up to be the best investigative reporter to ever work for the *Miami Herald*."

Reagan frowned. "Well, I'm an Assistant Editor now, but you know reporting is in my blood. Anyway, I was trying to wrap this up so I could come to Chicago, but I wasn't sure I could, so that's why I wasn't answering any of your texts or calls. When Dane I realized we needed to get out of Florida, I insisted that we come here. To *you*," she added.

"Landon, can you find somewhere we can hide?"

If you enjoyed meeting Landon and Kelsea St. Clair in *Home to You*, read their story in *Plan B*, available in print and eBook.

***

PLAN B

Kelsea and Landon have each been left at the altar, and neither has a Plan B. They decide to escape to the romantic island resort where they've booked a honeymoon, to hunker down in solitude. Enter Rose, a spry, pink-haired matchmaker, and watch the fun begin.

www.ingramcontent.com/pod-product-compliance
Lightning Source LLC
Chambersburg PA
CBHW022001170626
46808CB00001B/241